Just Like Wings

Avni A Madhwesh

Copyright © 2014 Avni Madhwesh

All rights reserved.

ISBN: 1495309711
ISBN-13: 978-1495309717

DEDICATION

To Nirupama and Anjan Madhwesh

CONTENTS

	Acknowledgments	i
	Prologue	1
1	The First Flight	3
2	School Again	6
3	Clouds And Mist	12
	Nadia Narrates	16
4	Galandor, I Need Your Help	18
	Galandor Narrates	25
5	Who Is She, What Is She, And Why Is She Here?	25
	Skylar Narrates	30
6	Do You Need To Know This? Is It Actually Necessary?	38
7	Back Home	42
8	Trouble	49
9	The Note	55
10	Wings	62

	King Elf Narrates	67
	Shira Narrates	68
	Skylar Narrates	71
	Nadia Narrates	76
	Logan Narrates	92
11	The War Begins	92
	Skylar Narrates	99
	Selina Narrates	121
	Skylar Narrates	126
12	The Arrow	134
13	A New Life And Beginnings	138
	About The Author	143

ACKNOWLEDGMENTS

This book would not have existed if it wasn't for my parents Nirupama and Anjan for encouraging me to write and for helping me to edit my book. Thanks to my friends Celeste, Shira and Selina for encouraging me and lending their names! Thanks also to my extended family who gave me great feedback and encouragement and to my little sister Neha, who answered all of my weird questions. Last but not the least my teachers in Zurich International School who were very patient with me and guided me through entire development process.

Prologue

The day I discovered flying was a day as ordinary as a day could be. They say having an imagination is a great thing, but what if what you see is not really your imagination? Is that a good thing? Because that's what happened, and I only knew one person who understood that. And that was my grandmother.

****

I cradled my son's newborn baby in my arms. The baby girl was the third one. Born with the powers of the sky, and I was proud to be her grandmother. My days there were a long time ago.

Would she be like me… did she become like me… well of course she did. I would know it, dead or not. Her time was much more… complicated. And that is what's in this story.

Her name was Skylar Rose Harris, and I had asked for the name to be that. I knew she would soar, and the name seemed perfect.

And I was right. She did… but isn't this what the story's about?

So the story begins 13 years from now...

1- The First Flight

"Urgh!"

I pulled handfuls of my shaggy brown hair as I stormed up the stairs. This was probably the 5th time of the day - my family annoyed me - again. I love them and all, but sometimes they're embarrassing.

I slammed my door shut and sighed. I could still hear my little brothers thudding and throwing themselves against the wall in their fake wrestling match. Why was it me, with this miserable life, unpopularity at school, embarrassing braces, irritating 7 year old brothers that call me names like "metal mouth". Sometimes I wish I could fly away like a bird, swift in the wind.

I walked up to my bedroom window, opened it, and sat on the windowsill. I was all alone except for myself and my thoughts. I bent forward to check how far the ground was below me, (I stay on the 6th floor on a 7 story building) and I fell.

"EEEEEK!" I shrieked as I braced myself for the cold, hard, brick ground that lay below me. I squeezed my eyes shut so tight I could feel tears streaming upward as I fell. It was the end. Like the end of a fairytale when the princess lives happily ever after. Except not like that. My fairytale was ending in the exact opposite way. The end of everything I had ever loved, known and seen or heard! At least for me. As I was falling I must have gone a bit nutty because I was humming a song. The bit that goes like "and i'm lying on the cold hard ground. aaah". I dared myself to look down just to find that the ground was about 2 meters below me.

I readied myself to hit the ground but I felt nothing. I thought I had probably died. I was still curious, so I opened my eyes and I saw that I was soaring over my home. In New York City. I felt like I was dreaming.

It felt like nothing I had ever felt before! If it had actually been a dream, I would have said "Don't wake me up. It felt exactly like magic! I wish I could have just flown forever and ever and ever and ever and ever! That's 4 evers. Forever!

The adrenaline, the speed, the wind in my clothes and hair. I loved it soo much I could think of nothing else. I thought of flying through the night sky to reach for the bright moon. And if I had the chance, I would sit on it.

But I couldn't keep flying! I had to go home and return back to the miserable life I had left behind at my bedroom window. I was very tired already and had school the next day. I glimpsed at the skyscrapers and city lights, and heard the honks of anxious car drivers, tired of the traffic and exhausted from work and just wanting to go home to their families. I didn't want to go home. But I had no choice but to bid the deep blue sky and the dazzling stars farewell and sadly fly home.

    I came back and rapidly tucked myself in bed like a whirlwind, still in my day clothes. It was probably a good thing I had returned quickly, because as soon as I did my mom barged in, realized I was sleeping (not really) and left. I was pretty sure that this was some crazy dream and I would wake up as plain old Skylar.

2- School Again

"Skylar! Hurry up! The bus is almost here!" My mom yelled from the bottom of the stairs.

"COMING!!" I replied. Ok it wasn't entirely my fault I forgot to set my alarm for 6:30, like I normally do. I am hopeless in the morning. I woke up at 7:40, only 10 minutes before the bus comes.

"HONK!" honked the bus. I pulled my star printed curtains aside. When I looked down I found our normal yellow and black school bus, and along with it a very impatient bus driver, checking his watch. I pulled on my jacket, backpack and sports shoes, in such a rush that I was not able to tie my shoelaces.

Just as I was about to fling the front door open and flee down the stairs, my mom tossed my clarinet at me. It had totally slipped my mind that I had 3rd period music. My legs were too impatient and didn't let me stop to say thanks. I finally reached the entrance as my bus driver gave his remark.

"You're late," he said in his gruff voice.

"I know, I know," I answered as I jumped (or did I fly?) onto the bus. I walked down the aisle to the back seat where Shira greeted me. Shira had long wavy soft dark brown hair that went to her waist. She had cute wayfarer glasses which Miley the mean girl thought were nerd glasses because the lenses were big. Shira was tough, so she just said "How do you only have 49 pairs of designer jeans?" back. She normally wore sweatpants and a sweater with boots.

"You're late. Well technically, it's not completely your fault, because the bus driver was late to my stop and I was early and it's not exactly your fault that you live on the 6th floor of a 7 story building." she finished.

Shira loves to extend her sentences and is really smart and mature, unlike one of my friends, Selina. Selina loves to mess about in class and doesn't really care about getting in trouble. That is one thing Shira dislikes about Selina, but is still her friend, nevertheless.

"So…?"

"So you were late, but as first on the bus, I know that Jace was also late."

Shira and I chatted about classes, latest songs, and rubber band jewelry. We weren't really able to finish our conversation because within 15 minutes we reached the school. Shira and I were walking to our lockers when Miley and her bubble brain cronies passed us. Miley is the most popular girl in all of eighth grade. Everyone seems to adore her (including the teachers) .

We loaded our bags in our lockers and brought out what we needed for first period. "BRRIIINGG!" The bell rang and soon the hall was full of scurrying people going in all directions. I hate crowds. They make the place feel stuffy and I'm also claustrophobic and crowds close up the place.

My first period class was homeroom, where I met Selina.

"Hey, Selina," I said.

"Hiya, Skylar! Are you tired? You sure look like it."

"What?'

"You have bags under your eyes. You look a lot like you're aging. How old are you again?"

"13."

"Oh."

Our homeroom teacher entered the room. We all fell silent immediately. Even Selina. I guess the teacher was just kind of scary. And strict. And if we did something wrong while she was talking, she stopped talking and gave us the death stare.

Then she walked up to the front of the room and started asking for homeworks. OMG! (I don't normally say that. Miley says that) I had totally forgotten about the homework due that day! Of course, Miley, teachers' pet, walked up and was first to hand in the essay. Mrs

Amherst fell head over toe at the sight of it and gave Miley a shower of praise. As Miley passed by my seat, she flipped her golden hair in my face and held her nose.

I wasn't able to focus in class. I was thinking about flying the previous night when Selina leaned back in her seat and passed a note. It said:

How can she yammer on about her favorite way to solve complicated algebra for 30 min. straight. Isn't there a guinness record for this or something?

I replied: Not really listening

What?! You know we have to do an essay right?

Uh Oh

Yeah "uh oh"!

I really was worried now. Only 8:40 in the morning and my day was already a disaster. I had other plans for study hall.

"OK everybody, here are your essay sheets. I expect these to be done in 15 minutes. Right, Skylar?"

Yeah right. Ok maybe I am not the best time manager. I guess maybe once a while ago I stretched the time limit a bit and took 40 minutes more for a quiz than was allowed. My 2nd period art class teacher, Mr. Smith, wasn't happy and I had to sit back after hours to complete my assignments. Not to mention I was totally embarrassed. The 6th graders kept saying "Fail !!". Yet, despite my embarrassment, I couldn't hold back my laughter at their imitation of the 8th grade. To all the 8th graders, fail is the holy word (even to me). Their high pitched voices just kept reminding me of Ryan and Jason calling me "a fail". That isn't even grammatically correct - the word is failure.

"Yes Ma'am".

"Good. Now get cracking."

Homeroom seemed to drag on forever and I was not really expecting a very good grade from Mrs. Amherst. Mrs. Amherst was going to ask me a question about division but the bell rang. Saved by the bell. I walked out of the room to my locker where I met Shira again.

"Hi, Skylar."

"Hello Shira."

"Wanna walk to art together?"
"Sure."

After that, I did art and finished the whole day (almost), except something different happened during 3rd period, band. I was walking to band. You can always tell where band plays because more than half the grade plays in the band and they create a lot of noise. I opened the door and found a familiar sight. Saxophones, trumpets, french horn, percussion, flutes, clarinets, etc. I saw them putting instruments together and people rehearsing complicated pieces for the assembly. No-one was doing anything non-related to music. I went to my front row seat in between Sophie, one of the many flute players, and Sita, one of the clarinet players and sat down.

3- Clouds And Mist

La la la la la la ♪. I blew hard. Nothing came out. Not a sound. My face was turning red. I hated this song. But that wasn't the worst bit. Soon Ms. Harper approached the clarinet section.

"Now, clarinets. There is a new note you need to learn for your piece. Now play a normal F, the thumb on the upper body," Ms. Harper instructed.

"Duuun," the clarinets musically replied.

"A very nice sound, clarinets. Better than what I expected. Play F, and add the register key in."

It screeched when I played it. Ms. Harper instructed me to be brave and give it another shot. I did what she said but had a not-so-melodious sound come out and couldn't take it anymore and started coughing. She said I could go and take a drink as I exited the room.

I sat on the steps outside of the music room and thought hard about what I could do. I really didn't want to go back in there, if I could help it. In fact, I didn't feel like going any lesson at all. And then I had a mini light bulb in my head go ding! I realized I just wanted to go out and fly again. But there was still this part in my head that was freaked out about being able to fly! I don't even know if that was just a dream I had yesterday and I'm still an average, normal, unextraordinary girl who lives in New York City. But that didn't mean I couldn't go outside and give it a try.

I slowly and stealthily tiptoed to the back door which nobody actually uses. Once I was outside, I looked for the safest and secretest high ground I could find. I looked around the scattered- with- dry- autumn- red-orange and yellow leaves area. Every single bit of the building was covered with windows and if I even had moved a step, someone or the other would have caught me. Then I knew what I had to do. I had to climb the school building to reach the top of the school on the roof. I could then do whatever I needed to do because they didn't have windows up there.

The climbing was painful but I had finally reached the top. I stopped by the band room window to check if anyone had noticed my absence. Nope. I was in luck. I sighed with relief but forced myself to not stop and climb forward. Once I reached the top I realized how big the building was. But it was actually perfect for what I was about to do.

I also realized what I was I about to do on the roof of the building and its consequences. It would not be very good if my experiment didn't work! I was being very... erm... crazy. I was still not sure if I could actually fly. And the consequences of jumping off a roof would be possibly be death and even worse - a bad school report..

But something inside me was pretty cool about it. I just trusted this thing and I ran, and jumped. And screamed. And felt nothing. Again. A wave of all the thrill and emotions from last night washed over me. I was already feeling better. Now, I had the proof I could fly.

I still really didn't want to go back to class. I wanted to keep flying. And that is exactly what I did. I started to fly upward faster than I had flown before. I was flying so fast I couldn't really think. I was too astonished to even think about thinking. I was too astonished by the fact that I could even fly, and fly this fast.

"ZOOOM! WHOOSH! Plop". I had flown so far up that I couldn't see the ground. When I looked above me I just saw layers and layers of mist and cloud. I raised my arm to see if they were real. But I didn't feel water or dust (I know this because I had studied them in 4th grade), but I felt some soft, squishy stuff. I was pretty curious and I charged straight at it and landed on the other side.

I couldn't believe my eyes when I saw what I had discovered. There probably was no word in any dictionary that had ever been made to describe what I saw. It wasn't just clouds and birds and other stuff you would think people find in the sky because that is what you see on an airplane. It was nothing like that. It was an entire city built in the clouds!

There were shops, pools, (weird for a sky, I know) houses, even more-so in- the- sky skyscrapers, and even a palace (but it didn't look like a friendly palace. Instead of gold, shiny, and sparkly stuff on the outside, It was spiky and painted darker and scarier than a terrible storm at midnight. On the top largest spike there was a flag with a face of a king, who didn't look any kinder than the palace). Further away, there was a cloud mountain kind of thing with an actual rainbow liquid waterfall (more like a rainbow fall, if you ask me). There was sun shining everywhere, too! But that wasn't the best part. There also were people! Not just normal people, Fairies! With actual wings, and they were acting completely normal, minding their own business. There was so much to see, I felt like my eyes would pop out and become shooting stars!

I hadn't realized how flying had drained my energy away. I was starving and thirsty. Not just thirsty, but dehydrating. And then I collapsed on the spot.

Nadia

An outsider! A foreigner! How did she get here! I thought furiously. She was from below, where all those snobby wingless humans who keep shooting crazy airamabobers that disturb the cloud barrier and explode and create a horrible noise when our wings pierce them. Then you can't fly for a whole entire week and you have to get a wing cast. I cannot list how many times I have made that mistake.

I looked around the city square. Nobody had seemed to notice the midget human, or as we call them, Miroanalis. I gently fluttered my wings in the miroanalis's direction, cautiously, in case there were any of those explosion bomb airamabobers around. I wasn't going to risk my wings again. When I approached her I wondered if she was dead or asleep. She was probably dead because she was not mumbling and jumbling and saying funny stuff that have no use here. But she was still breathing. I picked her up and headed home, zooming so no-one sees. Fairies are not normally as snobby as the miroanalis that live below us so I was not worried that the other fairies would stop me to ask questions. Us fairies have studied the miroanalis for centuries and do not understand how they have not ceased to exist. We do not even know why they exist.

Us fairies, have lived much longer than Mironalis even before the Realms of the Sun was there. We lived in a different universe and came to a liking with the skies of many different planets as the Realms of the Sun came to be. The fairies made a big historical migration to the Realms. Many had died during the migration and some did not even migrate. The survivors came to be known as the Founders Of The Realms Of The Sun, the Founders Of Fairy Civilization. So then a new era of Fairies began, and was called the peace period.

My kind of fairies are based in the sun, so that's where we lived, until I decided to come to Earth. I found the earth to be perfect, not too cold, not too hot. But for the Iscilios fairies (the ice fairies), Neptune was better.

Many generation since, our small city in the Realm of the Clouds now blossoms with fairies. But this peace era will now be disturbed, for the miroanalis have attacked and bombarded with their weapons. They have even sent a messenger.

4- Galandor, I Need Your Help

She finally opened her eyes after an hour and asked: " Where is my mom? Want a chewy clarinet?"

And so I also had a very dumb reply for her. When you ask a dumb question, you get a dumb answer. So I said: "No, thank you. What is a clarinet, and which flavors does it come in?" I mean, who in the Realm Of Clouds would know what a clarinet is, except maybe Galandor the Great and Wise, keeper of the emerald stone, the power of skies, oceans, earth, and space and the only ancient powerful wizard still living and the librarian.

"It's a flute," she replied dreamily.

A flute. I did not know what that was either, but I did not ask in case she said it was another thing I didn't know.

I decided to take her to the doctor's office. But the distance was too long to fly with a dead but alive now midget miroanalis in my arms.

Then an idea made it's nest in my head. The idea sounded like something that would work, but it would also take a while.

I left the miroanalis safely in my house and started to fly away at my fastest pace. I went to retrieve my unicorn who spends her time dancing on rainbows. She never wants to sit still in her stall and always leaves for the rainbows instead. She is the best rider in the whole Realm and can get to the doctor's office in 5 minutes, but the rainbows are also very far away.

Way past midnight, I reached the rainbows even though I was flying at my fastest speed (the rainbows are always sunny. Night never falls there). I still don't know how she gets there so fast. I jumped on her back and extended my arm, wand too. I'm not a wizard, I'm a fairy sorceress. I have a limited knowledge of spells and it takes my kind longer than a normal wizard to learn.

"Ellectravincalia Miroanalis eliso elilsia housole!" I called in the Faioralalios language. It meant summon the miroanalis that's in my house. (It was the spell we used

for summoning something to come. You just shout Ellectravincalia and after that what you want to summon.) The summon part was the most important, but with this spell, anything could have gone wrong. For example, if I hadn't said *in my house*, the spell would have gotten any random human from below.

A white light arrived and faded away to reveal the dead- but- alive- but- dead- again miroanalis. "Ellictus!" I yelled. The miroanalis hovered in the air. As I moved my wand above Crystal, my unicorn, the miroanalis floated just above Crystal. "Tsswtp". She stopped hovering and dropped onto my unicorn. Crystal, not very experienced with avalanches, panicked and started into a gallop. "Steady, Crystal!! GENTLY!!!" I hollered. She was about to crash into the memorial statue of Queen Alexia the 6th. We had her statue near all the rainbows for a special purpose; to remind us of the golden age of when she ruled over us and the happiness she brought upon us. I'm sure she would understand if she knew my purpose. But she might not because with a dead- but- alive- but- dead- again miroanalis, an out- of- control unicorn, and all of this happening in the middle of the night, I wouldn't believe it myself.

 Crystal's hooves slid on the clouds as an attempt to stop. She abruptly jerked forward, hung her head down startled. Then she turned her head so she could look at me. She looked all innocent and stared straight into my eyes with her black beady eyes. She showed her thoughts to me. Since unicorns cannot speak, they think to us fairies.

Did I do anything wrong?

No, Crystal.

I feel like I did something wrong. I apologise.

Nothing is wrong. We need to consult the doctor for the miroanalis.

You have a miroanalis? This is terrible! Destroy it now! Before it is too late!

I cannot risk it. There is something different about her. I didn't go down and bring her. She came here by herself. And then she died.

Doctor Parthalamis's office will have probably closed. If it has not, we should go to Galandor.

Good Idea. Gallop, Crystal. But keep a steady pace.

She started to gallop. Tap, tock tick was the sound of her hooves clashing against the cloud ground surface. In a matter of seconds it began to pour. We reached just after 5 minutes of pacing. I hopped off Crystal, not bothering to take the miroanalis or fly. I ran to the door and saw a closed sign. And another sign that said that patients should not come before or after the office hours. Then I turned to leave, but accidentally pressed a big green button. A small hologram appeared on the button. A hologram of Doctor Parthalamis.

"Nadia? Is that you? You are knocking on my door at midnight and you brought Crystal with you? If she is not well, the vet is that way," he said, pointing.

"Doctor Parthalamis, I do not need to see the vet. I am sorry I disturbed you."

"What do you want?"

"I do apologize... I am sorry I bothered you, and I must leave," I said, hopping onto Crystal and hurrying away. I did not want to discuss miroanalis with a hologram.

We reached the library in a matter of seconds. I hopped off Crystal and tip- toed up to the red painted wooden door and reached for the golden rusty door knocker. Before I could even lay a finger on the knocker, the door was opened by Galandor the Great and Wise himself. I immediately recognized him. His bushy, white as snow hair and beard (tangled, I do say so myself), frosty blue eyes, lots of wrinkles, sharp nose and pink lips were all too familiar to me. He was wearing the usual star patterned hat and robe with small bells stitched on the edges and one on the tip of his pointy wizard hat. His staff was missing and I assumed it was inside.

"Nadia? Nadia! This late at night?" he asked in his powerful voice. He has known me since I was born and my parents were his good friends. When my parents went on trips, Galandor took care of me and reads books in the Library to me. This is the ancient library, full of valuable scrolls, treasuries, and history books, and anything else that has been written since fairies discovered ink and parchment. That is also the reason why I get top marks in Fairy History.

"Galandor," I said in a serious tone. "This is very important and cannot be delayed by a second if I can help it."

His voice changed. "... Come in Nadia. And bring your problem with you.". Galandor gestured for me to sit on his couch. I took off the black wet cloak I was wearing and placed it by the couch.

I quickly walked back to Crystal. My hand swished in the air as I cast a spell.

"Ellictus!" The miroanalis hovered in the air. Galandor looked confused. Then I gently lowered the miroanalis inside on the couch.

"A miroanalis...how could-"

Before he could complete, she trembled and turned over. Galandor stuck out his arm and the staff, at the other side of the tree, zoomed at his arm. He grabbed the staff and pointed it at the miroanalis.

"What...what have you brought me? You went down and got it?"

Before I could answer, he shot a pale blue light at her. It circled around her, floating higher and higher, taking her with it. The higher it went, the more she struggled. Now she was almost at the top of the narrowing tree. But when I looked closer, she was stuck and struggling to breathe. She puffed some green smoke. The smoke turned into a shape. A rectangle like shape. Galandor took his flying board and stood on it. Galandor and I flew up to take a closer look. We had to duck to avoid shooting blue sparks and stars coming from the light and rays that held the miroanalis up.

It was not a rectangle, it was a picture frame. With King Elf's face on it. Galandor seemed startled. He lowered himself and the miroanalis.

"She senses the presence of King Elf". He said after a long silence.

Galandor the Great and Wise
5- Who Is She, What Is She, And Why Is She Here?

"But she is a miroanalis...She isn't a fairy. How? It is not technically possible, not genetically possible. She knows nothing of our land and there are not many chances that she has seen the Black Palace Of Terror, much less that she has seen the king him-" Nadia thought aloud.

"Nadia, I have read you many books, but there are a few left- they were not meant for your eyes yet but the time has arrived earlier, much earlier than I had expected."

I grabbed my staff and pointed it at the hidden trapdoor, concealed with a very strong magic lock. It was revealed and the book flew out, and landed gently on the table. It was a large, heavy, old and dusty book. I opened it and Nadia and I coughed.

"This," I said between coughs "is the book of the fairies. The name is deceiving, for it is also about any being that has ever lived."

I opened to halfway in the book. Right there was a section on Aeroanalis.

"So, what is your answer? Did you go and get her?"

"That's the crazy bit. She came by herself, she did. She died right on Magic Avenue, just in front of the fountain. I brought her here to save our land. So she would not destroy anything. "

"Oh Nadia, you act too much like a Solarian," I chuckled. "Now as I was saying, she has just fainted. It is in a miroanalis nature that they faint when they are tired."

"Galandor, what is a faint?"

" Nadia, it is a term the miroanalis use for becoming unconscious. Now, where was I? Oh, yes. She is not dead by any means although I can see why you thought she is dying. However, it seems possible that she is one of the rare aeroanalis. And that is what this section of this book is about. Now, I, in fact, do believe that your young mind is mature enough for this."

Nadia looked curiously at me as I got up to grab my reading glasses.

"You are *very* mature for your age. When I read it first, I was about 1100 years old! Ahem, where were we..."

"Aeroanalis," I continued, "are the rarest specimen known to Fairykind. Their history begins with King Arraculis of Solaria falling dramatically in love with Taylor Jones of Minnesota, Earth. When he told the fairies that he wished to marry a miroanalis, they disapproved and told him that he could only do that by becoming one of them and never return to any fairylands. Arraculis agreed. He cut off his wings and used his final magical charm to reach the earth. As all fairies learn when they are young, if you quit the fairy kind and change to a different form or being (quite hard to become something of a higher rank, such as a wizard or an angel), you lose all your fairy magic and power, and obviously your ability to fly and converse with and understand unicorns. Arraculis and Taylor Jones got married, and soon afterwards, Taylor became pregnant. Sadly, one month before the birth of their child, Arraculis died. All fairy kings are immortal, but Arraculis was very old already, and as miroanalis are mortal, that is what he had become. The child was born and lived his life without knowing anything about his father.

Taylor had always thought of Arraculis as an extraordinary man, but what she didn't know was that he had not a single drop of human blood in his body." I said and took a sip of water.

"But Galandor, why are you reading me the middle of the book and not from the beginning?" Nadia asked.

"Let me finish. Since Arraculis had the ability to fly, his son did too. The family carried on but only every 3rd offspring was a flying miroanalis, or a miroanalis who had the ability to fly. They were soon noticed by the ancient fairies and they called this the Rarity of the Miroanalis, or for short, an Aeroanalis."

"Are you suggesting that she, the miroanalis in this room with us, this mere midgit, is an Aeroanalis?"

"Not for sure, but I have a little suspicion. The last Aeroanalis known to fairy kind," I resumed "was Sadie Pete. We believe she has died and she is said to have lived in Brooklyn, New York."

"So she is an Aeroanalis!" Nadia exclaimed.

"Don't rush into conclusions just yet! We do not know if she came up in that huge something they, they below, call a hot air balloon. Or do you know?"

There was a long silence. Nadia's face was turning pale. She was fidgeting with her fingers and twisting her hair around her index finger. Than she finally said something.

"No, Galandor. I do not have the faintest idea." She said, much quieter than usual.

"Well, we will have to wait until she awakens. Entertain yourself, I do not have anything you teenagers are into these days. Why don't you check on Crystal, see if she is doing ok, because you are going to have to tell her we will be here quite a bit longer."

Nadia left the room.

Skylar

It was spinning. The whole world was spinning. It always does but this time, I could feel it. I tried to recall my place I was at last but my mind was not settling on anything. I just kept on spinning and spinning and spinning and spinning and spinning and spinning and- "OH JUST SOMEONE MAKE IT STOP!!! ALL I CAN SEE IS A BLUR OF RED, ORANGE GREEN BOLUE P-U-R-P-P-L-E AND NO-ONE IS CONSIDERATE, KIND, LOYAL HAPPY, BLAH BLIBBER- DI- GIBBER KIND ENOUGH TO EVEN LET ME KNOW YOU ARE THERE AND IF YOU WANT ME TO SAY THE ALPHABET THAN FINE CUZ A B C D E F G H I J K L M N O P Q R S T U V Y X Y W X Y Z NOW I KNOW ABCS SO JUST NO HO SERII!!!" I screamed. I can't really remember what I said after that.

I was so dizzy. I jolted upwards and the spinning stopped. Slowly my vision cleared and I came back to my senses. Or so I thought. I began to wonder whether I was really seeing and thinking properly. Because I thought I was floating in a library built into a tree. Like, how bizarre was that? But the funniest part was when I looked down. I rubbed my eyes and tried to look closer but I saw the same thing. It was kinda like some Gandalf Or Dumbledore dude except that he really didn't look that appealing or happy to me. I don't think he liked me. Beside him was the most beautiful girl I had ever seen, way prettier even than Miley. She had long locks of perfectly natural curly red hair that fell up to her waist. She had emerald colored eyes as bright as stars. She also had a dress where the top half was a color between pink and orange and she bottom half was a ruffled skirt, with a pattern of one ruffle pink the other orange. Her lower arm was covered in sparkly blue bangles all the way up to her elbows and ballet like shoes with the extending ribbons that swirled around her legs. Soon I realized, after studying her a little more, her arm was outstretched, with a wand and pointing at me!! Then I looked at the Gandalf guy and he held a long bar of entwined polished wood with carvings that held a crystal ball at the top and some shimmery blue smoke/powder sort of thing. His bar was also pointed at me.

A bolt of blue tinged electricity was shooting out of his bar and circling around me. I tried to stretch but the blue ball was not stretching any farther than the small shape it was already.

"Who are you and what do you want?" The Dumbledore dude's deep voice boomed.

Being tied down and unable to move or eat or drink made me angry enough to shout.

"I don't care about your measly questions, get me OUT OF HERE, Gandalf person thing!" I hollered.

"Who is this Gandalf you speak of?" The old man's face was twisted with confusion and anger at my outburst.

"GET THIS THING OFF ME!!" I screamed with anger.

"DO NOT DARE SPEAK TO ME LIKE THAT! I HAVE MORE POWER IN THE SMALLEST TINIEST TIP OF MY PINKIE FINGER THAN YOU AND ALL IN YOUR ARMY!"

"What army? I don't see anyone in this room except for you me and the serene FAIRY in the corner!!"

Yeah, ok, whatever, I guess I just kinda… you know maybe like….. only just now realized that she was an…um… fairy. No wonder she was so beautiful, she is a fairy so it is natural to be pretty and slim and have pretty wings while some of us humans are obese, have warts and pimples, and can barely jump.

"My name is Galandor, not any Dumble Dore or Gandalf whoever that is." Galandor stated.

"**GET ME OUT NOOOOOOOW!**" I shouted so rambunctiously it was most likely deafening, not bothering to react to what he said.

Startled, Galandor dropped the bar. The fairy's jaw hung open and looked like it had no hope of ever becoming normal again. Ever. The magic had stopped flowing and I fell to the ground, again, forgetting I could fly. I sat up on the ground and my hand smacked my head. I just saw wings and sticks circling around me and I shook my head, just as my curly coated retriever, brownie, does after she comes inside after a rainy day. I stood up, or at least made an attempt to, with my legs feeling like jelly and my brain still dizzy.

"What do you want from me??" I said, my voice quivering.

"I want to know everything," he said, putting a little more force into that last word.

I showed him my empty pockets. "Um... I don't have any money on me," I said inching away, as they were cornering me. "But, I do have some breath mints, and...Um...er... I'm pretty much broke anyway." I nervously giggled.

"I said I want to know everything, not *have* everything. Breath marks, shoelaces, young fairies are right, despite most of them are gangsters; the miroanalis are truly pathetic and they are definitely not humble, always longing for attention." He boomed.

I didn't know what a miroanalis was. Whatever it was, I felt bad for it. I didn't even know if I was one. Weird. This wizard dude must have been speaking about some kinda being or something or the other that I obviously didn't know about. Because of it's description, it sounded an awful lot like it was a human. Then the so called Galandor turned to the silent fairy.

"Jasilikif illsora Elkolasha de Kalif sor Salantia Miroanalis," he muttered to the fairy.
Her expression became all crooked. And for the first time tonight, she spoke.

"Elkolasha? Jasilikif des Soleil of the Salantia Miroanalis?" She questioned in her delicate voice. I knew they were speaking another language, Gibberish maybe, but did I hear English in there? I listened further.

"Yes they stiloalta thrivalanciel exiositos. They are located on the isilanaldo oas the kmedilatorasii oseansed on palanetio Neptuilio sully siocolo."

Now I was sure I heard some things in English but I still couldn't understand exactly *what* he was saying, but the 4th time around I understood what they were saying completely, except for one or 2 words I did not understand.

"But, Galandor. Getting to Neptune will not be a problem, but does the Miroanalis know she is a Miroanalis?

"She does not. But now she can understand every word I am speaking. Yes you heard it right she can understand the Faioralalios

language and this conversation is no longer private, as it was previously." He finished.

Aha! I felt like shouting out. They were speaking in a different language so it was private and so *I* wouldn't understand it. But I do understand, so it is no longer private. Uh Oh. I was eavesdropping. I hate eavesdropping, so...um...actually...whatever.

Then I realized this Galandor guy was now pointing his bar at me.

"I have the most power in the world. Actually, the power of the world and surrounding worlds, and I am not afraid to use it!"

I gulped. If he actually had all the power of the world, I was dead meat. So I tried my great escape. I opened the door quickly and flew fast as I could.
I kept flying but I was so thugged out I felt like I was going to faint. Again. But I kept on flying. It was my only hope. I wanted to escape before they conducted their crazy scientific experiments on me. So I flew higher and higher, arm out stretched as I flew, then I found a big hole punched through the clouds and I let go. I didn't care if I died because it would put an end to my misery. If I had to die, it would not be in a world of clouds with fairies and magic sticks everywhere around me. So I bid forever farewell to the sky, because I would never return.

I was just about to exit the cloud area ground thing when someone had yelled "Ellictus" and I hovered in the air. I immediately recognized that voice. My head swished to the direction of the big old tree which was magic because it had a library built into it. And there she was, the beautiful yet impish fairy, side kick of that Galandor guy, who some how keeps his voice loud all the time. Sure enough, the fairy named No- Name was there, pointing her elegantly carved wand with a swan design on it at me. She probably cast the spell. I was so annoyed. I mean, she should put herself in my shoes (even though she was much taller than me and probably would not be able to fit in my already torn shoes). I was about to escape and actually live my happily ever after (hopefully *not* with a prince) and never return or fly again. But who stopped me? Ms. No- Name.

"I cannot allow you to leave. We need answers, not breath mints," she said, her red curly locks of hair gently blowing from the gusts of wind that were spewing out of her wand from the spell.

"Set me free! America is a free country!" - I said panting and almost fainting again due to my escape attempt.

"Ms. Human-" Galandor started.

"I have a name." I interrupted between my heavy breaths

"Well what is-".

"Skylar, pleased to meet, not really though. At your service actually probably not really. I could probably survive without you."

"Ms. Skylar, we shall take you back to the library. Then your interview will begin."

6- Do You Need to Know This? Is it Actually Necessary?

So I grudgingly followed them back to the library; mainly because I had no choice. I would have left if I could. I tried to do something about this "situation", but it didn't work. I told myself that I'm going to try to try to try to try to do nothing. I said try to so many times, because how was I going to stand still and escape? It's not technically possible. So I could try, but I didn't keep my hopes high. After we reached they started asking questions.

"What is your name?" The Fairy asked, with a suspicious look.

"You already know. What is your name, Ms. No-Name?"

"Nadia. Now we will proceed. How old are you?"

"13."

"Oh. How did you come here?"

"I flew."

"How are you able to fly? You obviously do not have wings." Galandor questioned, one eyebrow raised.

"I dunno," I said, shrugging. "I was pretty much minding my own business and then y'all decide to capture me for these STUPID QUESTIONS!" I shouted, my face turning red and my voice hoarse from the shouting. If I was a cartoon, there would be steam coming out of my ears and my face would be a very angry Thomas the train. The only reason I mentioned that was because Ryan and Jason are overly obsessed with it.

"ANSWER THE QUESTION!" Galandor yelled back, his breath blowing me to the other side of the library built into a mammoth tree, pinning me to a bookshelf. He was now pointing his magic bar at me. It was probably the 9th time tonight. I wasn't really counting.

He does need those breath mints, I thought. But I knew the best thing to do was to was just answer his questions.

"Ok, I'll tell you," I gulped. I did not want anything to do with this man. "So last night I fell out of my window and I started flying - I don't know why or how. During school today I left so I could try it again and I came here."

"This place has a name: The Realm Of Clouds, but for short, is the ROC. Do you know anyone with the name Sadie Pete?" He asked.

"Grandma Sadie!" I exclaimed. Grandma Sadie was the best grandma ever. She cared for everyone and was always making donations to the world. I loved her apple pies. I could still hear her comforting voice in my head. I could smell the delicate odor of her perfume. I loved her the most and she had even told me that I am her favorite granddaughter. Until she died.

I cleared my throat. "Yes.. I did indeed know her," I said talking formally.

"And lastly, are you the third child in your family?" He questioned.

"Yes, because Madison is first (she lives in California and already has 2 babies), and 2nd is Zoey (she goes to the Auburn University in Alabama), Third is me, and Jason was born 1 minute before Ryan."

"We have gotten the information we need. Now on the count of 3, you will return home." The fairy said. "Since you are so desperate to go."

"But-"

"One,"

"What about-"

"Two,"

"But I really-"

"Three," she said, batting her eyelids and before I knew it, the area was becoming brighter and whiter and the whole place faded into a winter wonderland as I closed my eyes.

7- Back Home

I opened my eyes and found myself lying outside at the back part of the school. I checked my watch, noticing the sunlight. It read: 4:30. The road was flooded with familiar faces chatting, walking, listening to music while riding home. And then I noticed Miley and her bubble brain cronies following her as she sashayed over in my direction. With a smirk on her face. I pulled myself off the ground and brushed myself down. I grabbed my skateboard since I had missed the bus (I don't actually know how it got there) and pulled my phone out, stuck the earphones in my ears and tried to act normal, like I was never lying on the ground and didn't notice her coming. But it was already too late.

"Hey Dorkie Pie, I saw you and I was wondering if you were actually a vacuum, sucking the dirt."

"Yeah loser. Dorkie pie, yer stinkin up the sky," Miley's cronies chorused. Then they flipped their hair and made a star with their fingers. That's what they do when they are in sync. (BTW, their group is Miley, Avery, Alexis, and Kaydence + Lyra and Joy sometimes hang out with them).

"Whatevs. Anyway, your royal smelliness is taking up almost all of my personal space," She added in a squeaky voice. Which was weird considering there was a 5 foot distance between us. Then she sashayed back and left with her cronies.

The only one still at school was Stella, an all star basketball player. I don't know much about her, but this is what I know. Her team, The Red Hoopers, has won 18 and ½ championships (the ½ because her team had a tie with another team once). She competes against adults (she is as tall as them) and has been given an award from the President of USA.

She dribbled the ball and stood away from the net and attempted a what I think was a free throw. It worked. She threw her fists into the air and walked to the benches so she could have a drink.

"Hi Stella," I said, sitting on the seat beside hers.

"Hey Skylar," She said after swallowing. Her face was flushed bright red and her body was shiny with sweat. The air around her was also warm.

"Uh… what are you doing out here?" I asked. "Shouldn't you be home?"

"I have a basketball club after this, and I'm just practicing. The people are gonna vote who is gonna be guard, and want to be voted and become the best player in the league."

"I'd love to see you play, Stella, but I'm quite late already. See you tomorrow." I said.

"WAIT!" She called. "Selina, Shira, and Faith were waiting for you at study hall. They asked me where you were."

"Ah Ok. Thanks Stella." I said, skating away.

I felt guilty about ditching Selina, Shira, and Faith (Faith is my other friend). But there are some things people can't speak about with friends. Like flying.

I reached home after 20 minutes. Ryan and Jason were making a mess with toys on the floor and chasing their crazy car stuff around the house. They zoomed in front of me. Jason kept going, but Ryan stopped to say:

"You are in big trouble."

"Yeah like that is gonna help me much."

"Your problem, not mine," he saluted and marched away. I rolled my eyes. Brothers truly are weirdos (or worse).

First thing first, I was famished so went straight and scoured the kitchen pantry and ate a few sugary snacks.

Just then, Mom came into the kitchen. I tried to hide the snack bags and pull out a banana, but too late. She saw me in action. She stood there, hands on her hips, disapproving my choice of and food, and started scolding me in her usual style - ranting on and on about the same thing for like, years.

"Skylar, I got a call from your school. Your teacher mentioned that you had not submitted your homework. Then you didn't return to your music class so your teacher had to put your clarinet in the lost and found. Ms. Gibson, your PE teacher, said you did not attend PE despite being at school! And now you are home late! What's going on with you?..... And where is your backpack? Seriously, Skylar, you really need to organize yourself. You are thirteen now and in your senior year of middle school. I expect this sort of behavior from Jason and Ryan, not…"

Her voice trailed away and I only heard whispering. And then an image popped into my head. It wasn't really an image, it was more like a flash-forward, except it never happened. I know, difficult to explain.

In it, I was in the palace I had seen in the ROC. I was climbing up a spiral staircase, extending to the top of the highest tower. Each stair was separately carpeted with an eerie red velvet. And all I could hear was the stairs creaking when I stepped, and the sound of my footsteps echoing in the dark black hollow tower I was climbing up. The rest was silence. But not for long. Evil laughter and cackling was getting louder and louder as I went higher. After a whole hour, I reached the top, and there was a room where everything inside was ice. It was so cold I was getting hypothermia and there were icicles hanging from my earlobes, making them sag down so far they might have broken off. There were small snowflakes resting on my eyelashes, hair, and eyebrows. The whole room was carved out of ice and it was snowing inside the room but at the far end of the room, was an ice throne and it didn't look that comfy. And on it sat a very short man, about as tall as Ryan, ordering people (only other men) around. The man had ugly bug wings and a black crown atop his head. He had a rather circular head, with grey curly hair that looked like the kind of wig they wore back in London a long time ago. He had a ruby red robe, that was trailing on the ground. He wore an undershirt that looked as if it were made of snakeskin. He had a dark red pair of pants that looked more like leggings and he had a belt, bordered with gems. And there on his belt, was a dagger, put in a fine case, embedded again with jewels, and looked as if it was ready to kill. Though his features looked not so scary, I felt as if he had evil in his heart. Then I suddenly had a thought - did he have a heart?

Slaves were forcefully scattered around the place. Each had no hair and no wings, and were dressed in black robes. They were *humans*. They had severe hypothermia and were almost dying, and if they had the luxury I did, of having a bed, they would be on their deathbeds. They had one single cloth on them, one side of the cloak draped one one shoulder, the remaining twisting from their hips to the kneebone, leaving a bare, exposed chest, so thin all I could see were bones and thin as paper veins, and shins and bare feet. Suddenly, one slave's face turned even more white than it was before, and he struggled for air. He fell on his knees, and took his last breath. The whole room fell silent. I felt my heart sink. I only had seen people die in movies, but this seemed the scariest. Then the king's harsh, venomous voice broke the silence.

"I want a new slave. A healthy hatchling. And I've found one." He hissed, revealing perfect teeth, slightly pointy, forming an evil grin, looking in my direction. And after that happened, the last thing I heard a familiar voice screaming NOOOOOOOOO! And to my horror, it was mine.

I screamed aloud and ran to get away from that room and the king. Only that I realized after I ran that I was still in my house and in the middle of one of Mom's endless lectures. Big mistake.

"...Skylar, I will not take this behavior. I'm talking to you and you're running away. What I'm telling you is serious stuff! Missing school is not appropriate behaviour and you need to tell me if you have any problems at school. Skylar? Did you hear what I said?"

I had no strength to go back and have a discussion with her now. I stormed up the stairs just the way I had done the day before and slammed the door. Another mistake.

"Don't you go slamming the doors now!!" Mom called.

I didn't answer but instead wondered what I could do. Do my pending math and english homework? Sleep? Fly? No, not fly. Not to ROC. I never want to go there again.

So I finally sat down and finished my homework, and without a cheat sheet. It was actually easy.

Evaluate $(0.03)^3$

The answer is 0.000027

Evaluate $(1/2)^4$

The answer is 1/16

Then I did a few more problems which also were easy. I was finished and now bored, so I picked up the book we were supposed to read for English honors - "To Kill A Mockingbird."

I had finished reading most of that book earlier, since English is my strong and favorite subject, unlike math. So the reading comprehension part was pretty easy.

Having eaten several snacks, I decided to skip dinner, set an alarm for 6 AM and I slept.

8- Trouble

I stepped out. I inhaled the cool and moist air. I pulled my coat on tighter.
I got on the bus again that morning, making sure I was 5 minutes early. The bus driver seemed happy, but Shira sure didn't.

"Skylar, where were you yesterday? Selina and Faith and I kept waiting for you during study hall.." Suddenly her voice sounded robotic and this wasn't one of her accent imitations. She now had a wand in her hand poking my throat. Her eyes flashed red and then a black glow went around the eyes. Her hair flew backwards, along with her glasses, just the way Nadia's did, except with more force. A red bolt of light circled me and I began to feel weak, as if the red was a pesticide.

By this time the whole bus was looking at us, in the back seat, including the bus driver. Everyone's jaw was hanging, as if hanging by a string, and the bus drivers cigarette fell down. But he didn't seem to notice. Shira then dropped her wand, and shrunk away from me.

"I… i'm so-o-rry-ee… it just," she managed to croak in a tiny voice, eyes pale blue and the glow fading away. The red had completely vanished. Her voice wasn't robotic anymore.

I was still shocked. I couldn't make out if what I saw was real - I had seen so many real - unreal things in the last few hours, but they were all in the ROC. This was probably my imagination I thought.

The whole bus was staring in my direction, probably expecting me to say or do something. The bus driver, had still not woken from his trance and I checked my watch. 7:20. Yikes! 20 whole minutes late. It was obvious this bus driver was not going to help me so I hopped off the bus, grabbed my skateboard, and zoomed off.

Shira reached the East side middle school, very crowded with all students, 6th graders, 7th graders, and 8th graders, 5 minutes after I did. She stuck her head in her locker and I heard a sniff.

"Are you okay?" I asked.

"Yeah I *cough* just have cold," she said, voice hoarse, and ending her sentence with a fake sneeze.

Sigh. Shira may be good at fighting back with Miley, but she sure wasn't good at lying.

"Shira, look, I am sorry about yesterday. It just-"

"Why should you be sorry? I'm sorry about what I did this morning." She said, turning around. And the next second, her jaw fell open. Then she closed her jaw and started blushing uncontrollably until her face became princess Aurora's rose.

I turned around to see what Shira was looking at and I saw Logan Hare. Lots of people liked Logan, especially Miley, but I never knew Shira liked him. He was really popular and the best electric guitarist in our school. At least he bacame it after he won the 6th grade talent show. He was popular without trying to be so, unlike Miley and her cronies, plus a few other people like Kaitlyn.

Just then, Miley goodie 2 shoes, (actually everyone has 2 shoes) whose locker was next to Selina's (Selina's locker was on the other side of the hall), slammed her locker door shut and floated over to Logan, who just acted like he didn't know her. Selina, who was very used to Miley's slamming lockers, covered her ears just as Miley reached Logan.

"Logie, I will be a second, but you can go to history without me." Miley chirped, flipped her long straightened golden hair, adjusted her lip gloss and sideswept bangs for the second time today, and in her designer flats came clacking towards us.

Me and Shira tried to escape the Miley torture, but slammed into our lockers instead, stumbled and dropped our books and papers at Miley's feet.

"OWW!! You just RUINED my whole autumn outfit from the latest fashion line of Prada! Even my new hot pink tote won't look good! All because of this rash you pests caused me. I need to change into my UGG boots now! With a whole new featured outfit from Guess! With my other Gucci tote and Chanel jewelery which would mis-match!" She shrieked, gaping at my mismatched converse low tops. Personally, in all those designer brands of which I forgot the names, how could she complain of looking bad? Most of the times I get my clothes from Target and Walmart and only on special occasions, I shop at JCPenney or Kohls! And Shira shops at Macys.

But of course, when Miss America Miley is trying to say something in private and even if she screeches or makes a nasty remark, no-one seems to notice (even in a silent hall that echoes or something).

"As I was going to say, you guys will do better to STAY AWAY from me and Logan! We are going through a serious stage and you cannot ruin *another* thing near as important as clothing!" She remarked.

I had to stick my fist in my mouth to stop me from throwing up at that last sentence. Shira gagged.

"Mind your own honey scented beeswax. Get cracking before those people see that *designer* paper cut of y'all's," Shira imitated Mrs. Amherst and tried to speak Texan at the same time.

"Spoil my day, and I'll make you pay for it! Literally!!" Miley threatened. Yeah, like what will you do? Prank us? I just rolled my eyes. Shira must have read my mind, though.

"Yeh, Yeh," She said in a Scottish accent."What is the worst you could possibly do? Teachers won't really care about us sabotaging relationships." Shira finished. Now she was starting to sound like Selina, always joking around.

"Huh? Whatever. I am getting a migraine from you dweebs." Miley said, flipping her straightened gold hair in our faces. Normally that is what Stella calls the "midget 6th graders".

Just then I saw Selina looking worriedly at us and I remembered why.

A long time ago, in 1st grade, when Shira wasn't here, Selina had a crush on this boy called Deandre. He was really popular, as popular as Logan is now. So one day, she was telling her old friends Kaydence and Avery about her crush at the time during lunch time. Miley ended up eavesdropping on them as she was carrying her lunch to the table. Miley who had chubby cheeks then but the same hair (except shoulder length and curly) and same ocean blue eyes asked what was going on, but Selina didn't tell. But when Selina's head was turned, Kaydence told Miley about Deandre. The next day, Miley shouted it out and Selina has never spoken to her since.

Annoying Miley, a whole 2 month grounding from my mom and trying to hide the fact that I could fly, I knew I was in trouble.

9- The Note

I was sitting down at my French class with Miley, Shira, Logan, when I got a note in beautiful handwriting from Miley.

Do you want to go out Friday night?

Miley

What?! Why would I- oh, for Logan. So I passed it to Logan. And he wrote a note back for her on the other side.

No. I have **plans**.

I passed the note to Shira so she could see it. She ripped another piece of paper and wrote to me.

What?!

Yeah, I know. Should I give it to Miley?

Oh Definitely :D

So I gave the note back to Miley and then she turned around and scowled at me.

"I know you wrote that! Logan would never say no to **moi**!! She whisper-hissed at me, but said the moi loud enough for the teacher to hear so that she would hear on purpose.

"Miley! Qu'est-ce excellent (I forgot what she said here) Bientot, nous aurons parfaire à la conjugaison des verbes aussi! Bravo!" She said. I didn't understand a word except for perfect and excellent.

When she turned around and resumed her French, Logan piped in.

"Um, I actually have drum rehearsals friday afternoon. So..er..yeah." He finished and the whole class heard except for the teacher. Miley turned red like a fully ripe tomato in July. Everyone was smirking. But Miley never gets embarrassed. So she gave the death stare and everyone quieted down. Just then the bell rang and we all dismissed ourselves.

At the lockers, I met Shira, Selina, and Faith, and they were all wondering where I had gone.

"You guys, does it matter? I don't think it does."

"It does," they all chorused. Even Shira joined in.

"Ok, fine. I went flying in a city with quiet fairies and angry wizards that live on a giant cloud."

"You did WHAT!?" Selina exclaimed. Everyone in the hall froze and looked at me. Shira looked at me at first as if I was making up a silly story, but then her expression changed as if she knew what I was talking about but she didn't want to believe me.

"I er..slept." I stammered. Then everyone other than my friends got back to their personal business and the hall flooded with chatter once more. But my friends didn't believe me.

"Skylar, can we please just have the truth?" said Selina.

"Guys, what I said earlier was actually the truth, I can fly. And I need to know why. And last time was also the first time I...." my voice trailed away and I began to wonder why Galandor and Nadia were asking me all those mysterious questions and how they knew about grandma Sadie.

"What?" They asked at the same time.

"And then I fainted in the clouds and so I didn't come back until the end of school… No. More. Questions." I said frustratedly, hoping they'd understand. They did well enough to ask questions, but they didn't ask anymore, but they also didn't make the magic zipper on their mouths, as I was hoping they would. I also decided to leave out the rest of the story, saying I was gonna take off again and probably not come back until 6th period in Ms. Susan's history class.

"Yeah right. Snap out of fairytale world, Skylar. We want to know the truth, but you obviously don't care. This is wasting our time." Shira said.

"No, you don't understand! I am telling the truth-"

"Of course you're not. Do you think we're so dumb we can't make out you're speaking nonsense? Trust me, you might not notice it, but we can. I guess you had something so private you can't even tell your own best friends." Faith interrupted me.

"Would you please shut up and listen! I can fly, you're just don't want to believe me.."

"Just forget about it! We're already late for our classes, and the bell rang already! And you know what, only when you're ready to tell the truth, you can come back and talk to us" Shira said, and they all walked away. I watched their shoes and Shira's boots with the wand, clacking away in the deserted, empty, echoing hall and turn around the corner.

I felt as if a needle had pierced my heart at the thought that they would never be my friends again. I was telling them the truth.. Didn't they understand? Oh wait, they didn't *want* to understand because *they* can't fly. The needle dug further but I pulled it out. Was this the feeling of betrayal? Probably. It must be. I needed to forget, not forgive and just move on.

As I got up to walk to my next class, I pushed all thoughts about my friends aside, and imagined I was flying high, and as I did this, my heart began to heal. Adapting a tough skin, I guess? I laughed at my own joke. I grabbed my language book and headed towards room EO640.

I sneaked through the door and tried to blend in and pretend I was always there, but too bad. Ms. Amherst had already noticed first my absence and then presence.

"Skylar, 10 minutes late. 10 minutes!" Ms. Amherst said with a angry hint in her voice. "My class isn't a get-up-

and-leave-and-come-back-whenever-you-want-to class!" She said with a furious tone, eyeballing Dylan Brown, who was simply getting up for a tissue. Dylan's face turned from calm to frightened, and he slunk back into his seat. If we disliked Ms. Amherst, Dylan detested her. If we were scared by her, Dylan was terrorized by her. For sure, each time he sees Ms. Amherst, his day is ruined (practically everyday and all the time), and he doesn't answer any questions (practically everyday and all the time) even though he is really smart and gets straight As.

"I expect better time management from a 6th grader. And-"

"Can we start now?" Kaydence asked in an annoyed tone.

"Yes, Kaydence! Class, pull out your language books, write the date, October 30th, 2013. (I was born in 2000, and my birthday is October 17th), and the learning object is to write a draft for a persuasion test". I raised my arm.

"Now you may begin your introduction - Skylar, what now?"

"I feel like I am going to be sick!" I groaned, running out the door as the class followed me with their eyes. Kaydence scoffed and rolled her eyes. Others just ignored. But I left before Ms. Amherst told me I could leave. I ran to the bathroom and sighed. I had a gift for lying and acting. I don't normally do that, but I guess I needed to. If it meant I get to see the skies again. My curiosity was too much and I ran across the bathroom and jumped out the open window and immediately went upwards extremely fast.

10- Wings

I zoomed upwards, enjoying and relishing the cool autumn temperature, a big relief from the stuffy classroom I was crammed into just minutes ago. I was determined to find the fairy, Nadia. I whizzed and broke through clouds. In a matter of seconds, a colossal shadow covered me as if it were the black cloak I had spotted in the library built into a tree, which was also big. I looked above me, and there was the ROC (it was still daytime). But I had no time to admire it, I had to run. I couldn't let any fairies see me. So I ran until I found the tree. I looked to the tree's sides, and I saw a unicorn sitting there, looking at me, as if it saw me before. It was a pink fluffy one that had a long, golden, curly mane. It had a dark blue vest on it that had glowing yellow stars, and it had a hem of rainbow swirls, carefully embroidered, and in cursive writing, in the color of fresh snow it said:

Crystal

As soon as I read it, the old wooden door of the library built into a tree opened, and Nadia stepped out.

"Nadia!" I cried. She threw her hands up in shock. She looked around, her hair whooshing through the air. She beckoned me, but when I came, she grabbed me by the collar of my shirt.

"You miroanalis! We sent you down last night and hoped you wouldn't return. Now why are you here? We need to get this over with before someone spots us." She whispered.

I have my reasons to be here, but it will take a lot of time to say and I can't be late, like last time." I said, using my flying strength to pry away from her grip. She dropped me and pulled out her wand and it immediately reminded me of Shira's wand. She squeezed her eyes shut and muttered an incantation. While she said more words, a clock appeared out of nowhere (actually, out of her wand) and sunk through the cloud ground and headed towards the ground of earth. Nadia opened her eyes, revealing jade colored pupils, and said this.

"Below, I have slowed time by much. Teenage fairies are normally not able, or even the best of adult magicians, are not able to perform such a complicated spell. But I am the Fate's time daughter for the Sun Realm, or Solaria for short. That means I have the ability to control time anywhere any time. Now, what are your problems? Don't tell me yet, give me a second. *Sylvioal!!*" She shouted, her wand pointed skyward, and a bright light captured my vision, and a second later, my vision returned and I found myself in a friendly looking shop, with a friendly looking woman with blond curls in a bun with orange wings and a pink dress with a tutu.

"Hello Nadia!! Good heavens, where have you been- huuuuhhh! Is that a..."

"Beth! You must understand! This miroanalis needs to blend! For our own sake, will you find her out-joint wings, please?" Nadia said impatiently. Beth thought for a while.

"But King Elf-"

"Beth, please. Put the blame on me." Nadia was practically begging.

".... I will see what I can do." Beth sighed.

"Stay on the ground." Nadia whispered in my ear. So I sat down as Nadia flew up to Beth in the wing section. Seconds later, they returned with a pair of wings. Beth took the pair, and Nadia grabbed my shoulders to keep me still. Something happened and I had a pair of wings attached to my back. I felt a slap and a magical whizz and I panicked.

"What.. What's going on?" I screamed.

"Calm down, nothing's happened. Just stay calm, nothing happened." Nadia fluttered her rainbow colored wings and dragged a mirror in front of me and I gasped. Bright blue, purple, magenta, emerald hem, sparkly wings... On *me*. It just looked so weird with my normal clothes and face, and for once in my life, I felt beauty conscious. My face was not fairy-like, my hair was neither, and my clothes had no style whatsoever. Even though I hate fashion and Miley's annoying sayings in in class like 'fashion is my passion!', my face gave my thoughts away and Nadia noticed.

"Beth, can we make her more Fairy?" Nadia questioned, winking at her.

"You don't need to ask me twice!" A big grin spread across Beth's face. Nadia flew over and grabbed my arm.

"Whah?.. let go!" But she had already dragged me into a mysterious room hidden at the back of the shop.

The whole room was filled with fairy outfits plus shoes and purses. There was a female section and a male section. She pulled me into the female collection of clothes with Beth trailing behind us. Then Beth stopped and I was pulled into another room by Nadia. It was a rather small room but the walls were mirrors and there was a huge shelf , more like a vanity, and a beautifully decorated chair with a red cushion.

"Come, sit." Nadia chirped. Not knowing what would happen next, I sat down as a blindfold blocked my vision.

Fairy King Elf

Anger.

Sorrow.

Evil.

A mixture of all flooded my heart. If I had one. A miroanalis. Has entered my own. But an Aeroanalis. A one of a generation. Of all. I long to fight. For myself. For me. And I. With an army of the Elkolasha. I am prepared. For all. Bring what you will, for I am undefeatable. Invincible. Endless.

Shira

I can't believe it. I walked away from Skylar. My friend! So close almost family! But it wasn't my fault. How could she not tell me! How could she not tell me? But I regret what happened this morning, with the wand. Okay, that is my biggest secret - that I am a sorceress. My mom is a normal person who has no unique talents except for flipping pancakes and having them land back in the pan instead of Drake's face. The only things my dad is good at is history, technology, (although sometimes I have to remind him that you have to press both the lock button and the home button at the same time on an iPad to get a screenshot, and not first the lock button then the home button!) joking, and understanding movies. Drake, my big brother, who is 15 years old, is good about freaking out about his iPhone and when his fingerprints are on it. Jake, who is 17, is good at getting really mad and swearing and driving away and killing bunnies (he once drove on a bunny). And my 6 year old sister, Casey, is good at holding her breath until she get things her way. And me, I'm good at nothing. I'm clumsy, boring, have no talents, can't hold a pencil right, never learned how to type and am a brace face. Except, I am a sorceress. I always have my wand in my boot, and at home, it's in my pocket. Drake always says I like carrying *sticks* around because I think they will give me good luck, which is so not true. I use it to perform spells from my spellbooks. My favorite spell is the summoning spell, Ellectravincalia, because I can get anything I want. Like how I summoned a pair of UGGs

(I'm not sure where they came from though!) My mom, when she saw them, said she never bought me UGGs before and she was never able to afford them for herself, but after a while she agreed that maybe her memory wasn't fresh anymore, but I'm not just an average sorceress, I'm also a pretty decent liar. But I have to make sure not to become spoilt. So I secretly go to a place called the Realm Of Clouds for sorcery practice from the most amazing wizard, Galandor the Great and Wise, keeper of the emerald stone, the power of skies, oceans, earth, and space and the only powerful wizard still living and the librarian. He knows I am another one of his Fate's child, in this case a daughter, representative of land, and after Nadia, his ultimate pupil. This all links to Skylar saying stuff about quiet fairies and angry wizards that live on a giant cloud, but I think she must be imagining. Surely she couldn't fly!

I was walking to choir with Faith. "Do you think she can really fly, or could she be lying to us?" Faith asked, after a long silence.

"No. I don't believe she can fly. It is hard to believe that she can lie, but it is easier to believe that than imagining her fly," I replied briskly. She didn't ask anymore questions. Then I stared at her, as I realized that it was harder for her, much harder. She knew Skylar more than I did. She knew her secrets. Skylar has her own special place in Faith's heart. Faith looked crushed and about to cry.

I suddenly realized that I made such a rude statement about Skylar, while I have been hiding stuff from my friends myself. And I felt guilty. Very guilty. I didn't want to go to choir any more, I just wanted to have my friends with me again.

I met Ms. Spencer and singing voices as soon as I opened the door. Ms. Spencer is normally nice and happy and talks musically, but today she was mad.

"We waited for 7 minutes for you to come! I am normally OK with 30 seconds late, but I know from working here for 9 years and teaching you for 3 years, your hearing is perfectly fine and the bells are- in fact, too loud." she said, shaking her head as if the memory of the deafening bell was stuck in her head and traumatizing her.

I walked into the room, not feeling ashamed or sorry. Faith stayed back, apologizing. I took my seat. Stella, who sat next to me, scowled.

"I hate waiting!" She said. "I could have won a championship in that time!"

"I know how you feel, Skylar showed me," I said, remembering all the times she was late to the bus.

Skylar

I opened my eyes and gasped at my appearance. I was.. I was.. pretty. I had long, wavy, *blond* hair. All the same length! My bangs were somehow swept to one side perfectly, not a strand falling on my eyes, as it normally does. A small, short, curled section of my now blond hair fell to the side of my perfectly shaped head. The remaining bits and pieces were made into a side fishtail. My eyes were sky blue. I had my ears pierced. My nose looked different. My lips were pink and perfectly fitted on my jaw. And when I opened my mouth, braces had vanished! My teeth were white and shiny, and all the same height and at the same position. I looked like a model. But I still had my normal clothes on. With those on, I looked so weird.

Nadia smiled at me. Just then, Beth barged in with an outfit that matched my wings. She looked at Nadia, and then me, and Nadia, and me, and before I could say anything, I was thrown into a changing room. When I came out, Beth's jaw fell open.

"Nadia, are we looking at the same person?" she chimed.

"Indeed. Thank you for your help." Nadia smiled, raised her wand and.. WHOOSH! She cast a spell that took us back to the library built into a tree.

"Now, before we had gone there, you said you had some things you needed to tell me about." Nadia whispered. I pulled my jaw back into normal position. Just a few minutes ago, I had just reached, and now, I'm a fairy. I was shocked. Maybe I had underestimated Nadia's power.

"I don't think it's safe to say it out here. Do you have a safe place for secrets?" I whisper asked back.

"I do. Follow me," Nadia said gently. So I followed her. We went through twists and turns out into a big forest. We walked a little further to a bush and she pushed the bush aside. There was a hole in the ground that seemed like it only had space for half of my body. But Nadia, taller than Stella, went straight into the hole. Then she popped her head out. "Come on, what are you waiting for?" She asked. She pulled her head back in and I, not knowing what to do, followed her. But when I entered, I didn't enter a hole, I slid through a long slide (like the ones in amusement parks) and I plopped straight onto a soft pillow. I looked up and saw that I was in what looked like a palace. Nadia was standing there. I was awestruck at the palace. Then I looked at Nadia. She looked pleased. She looked like the queen of the ROC and deserved to be it.

"Not much, but it works like a gem. Now, would you like some tea?" She asked.

"No thanks. But I would like to speak to you." I replied, now getting really ticked. I just wanted a chance to tell her about everything, but she keeps going off topic.

"Oh yes. Have a seat." She pointed to a red velvet couch. I ruffled my skirt and sat down.

"Um.. I was just wondering why you were asking those questions last uh.. night." I asked.

"Well, I'm not sure if I should tell you this freely, but it is not good to leave people curious when the answer is with you. So we believe, since you flew here without any help, that you are from the long line of the Rarity of the Aeroanalis. I am not sure you know this, but an Aeroanalis is a human with the ability to fly, just as us fairies do. Only every third child from the family of the Aeroanalis is the one who can fly. Those answers you gave us, confirmed our suspicions. You *are* an Aeroanalis. A one of a kind from an ancient line. You are the only living descendant of our most cherished king, well, prince when he left, Arraculis. You were born with a connection to us, your destiny linked with ours." She said with pride in the last sentence. She was obviously grateful to be fairy.

"I.. I had a vision. Of an evil king in a frozen ballroom, ordering slaves, at the top of a black castle." I said, hoping she would tell me it was just my imagination. But life in the sky doesn't work that way.

"King Elf! This is bad, Skylar. He senses your presence and he is determined to destroy any kind that does not appeal to him or even though he is afraid to admit it, he is jealous of! He is especially jealous of you because you are one of a kind. You are special. More than he is. A war is about to arrive, I can feel it. He is ready." She said worriedly.

"Does that mean that I have to leave forever?" I asked. I had grown to like this place, and now I have to leave it. Leave it just as a war began. Well if I do have the abilities of fairies, I'm sure I can fight like one too. Fight for them.

"It would be good If you did, for you are the cause of war." She answered. I guess war was enough to send an Aeroanalis away. But not forever.

"Well too bad, I'm staying. I have the ability of a fairy-" I was interrupted.

"Actually, you are part fairy. What happened was a fairy married a human and had 3 children, so you are part fairy." She said.

"WHAT?!?" I was so confused. "Okay then I'm 1 googleth 1 percent fairy then. But I can fly like you, and I can fight like you, so I can obviously be a help to your team. Think about it, Nadia. If you really want king Elf dusted and gone, you will need all the help you can get. If I am the cause of war, does that mean I cannot fight the war? The only reason I haven't already left is because I like this place, and I would hate to leave it at the brink of war. I will fight, whether you like it or not." I said boldly, showing her I had no intention of leaving whatsoever.

"Fine, come with me. If you want to fight." She whispered. She pulled her wand out of her shiny belt pocket, made just for her wand as it fitted ever so perfectly. Her arm swished in the air. "Ellectravincalia Crystal!" And before I realized, the same pink fluffy unicorn I had seen earlier had returned.

Nadia

I brought Crystal using my wand. Skylar looked astonished.

"Well what are you waiting for? Hop on." I asked her. She started to climb. "You can fly," I said, astonished that she forgot that.

"Oops," she said, flying without using her wings. Crystal took off immediately.

"Skylar, if you want people to believe you are a fairy then you must act like one. Flutter your wings as you fly. Actually, *use* your wings. We are going to Harkinsailo's wand shop. There we will find your wand." I said.

We rode across the forest, passed the library and rode further. Crystal knew where we needed to go, so I was not focusing on guiding her to Harkinsailo's shop. Skylar's fishtail was blowing in the air as she was admiring the rainbow falls as we passed them. Normally, the sprinkle of the fall gets on us and the side that was facing the wall becomes rainbow tinted. Crystal abruptly stopped. I opened my mind to hers. A confused look approached Skylar's face.

Crystal, is something wrong?

Yes. There is a rainbow.

We need to leave.

Please?

But-

Please?

This time there was a longing, an eagerness to meet her fellow rainbow. I jumped off of her so I could see her face clearly. Her eyes were looking into the distance, at the rainbow. Her head turned and it was evil. Her eyes were glowing red and her skin changed from pink to black. I only saw her eyes. Her mouth opened, showing fangs.

"Raarilia! Mo RAARILIA! Ileiolicallst! Ileiolicallavst dieorist ELICOROLIO!!" She spoke in the fairy language. She said: Rainbow! My RAINBOW! I! I want NOW!!

I replied calmly. *"Espilicilo parthilia leavilo elicorolio. Wilistia illicalia leliakia."*
"The more you complain, the more I will scold you. I leave now. We are late," I said.
If I hadn't known her since I was 4, I would have panicked. Just like Skylar was at that moment. She was inching away, and there was a 15 foot distance between us and her. But why? It may be hard to understand unicorns, but that's what they do when the want something and don't get it. They can even talk.

Then Crystal became normal again. She stopped and gazed at Skylar. She turned to me and cocked her head in one angle.

An Aeroanalis? The last living descendant?

Mhm...

But.. King Elf? He will... her voice faded into the distance. I already knew what she was saying. *He will kill.* I knew it. But I had to do all I could. To save us.

I hopped on Crystal, urging her to leave.

We will leave now. She started galloping away from the rainbow falls, understandingly. Away she galloped. Skylar had hopped on as well. She looked ahead. But I looked above, at the sun. In the skies the sun is bright, brighter than below, but us fairies have adapted eyes. We have the ability to look into it. I remembered my home. In the sun. Far away. Tears flooded my eyes. I remembered my parents. And how they died.

Long ago, someone broke into our house. A king without a heart. Using the dark of night as a cover, he struck. The door creaked open and a silhouette popped in. Night does come in the Sun, when one of the 16 moons take cover. That night, it was the Murderilia moon. The murder moon. He floated up the stairs. He walked into my parent's bedroom. He pulled out his blade and held it above his head, ready to strike. *Slice!* My mother was gone. So was my father. He left the house, as quiet as a mantis, quick and silent. The next morning, I went to their room. Their bed was colored red, and so were they. They were dead. I fell to my knees and sobbed. Elliah, my little sister, had ran to her room, and when I went to her room, she was gone.. Never had I felt worse. My parents had been murdered, my sister was missing. I ran away from home, hoping to forget, and left for the ROC, and I never returned.

I squeezed my eyes shut, trying to blink the tears away. When I opened my eyes we were already at the city square, in front of a dusty shop with the title: Harkinsailo's wand shop. I pushed the door open and walked straight to Harkinsailo's desk.

"She needs a wand," I said, pointing to Skylar, not bothering to say hello.

"What about a proper hello? Well, what wand does she-"

"I need a wand that is fit for an Aeroanalis," Skylar interrupted. Harkinsailo looked shocked. He probably wasn't used to people he has never seen before come to his shop and demand one of the most powerful wands.

"Just a second, please." he stammered. Harkinsailo, age 95, hobbled out of the room. He arrived a minute later, holding a slim wooden case gently. It had an angel's wing with a halo floating above carved on it. It meant it was designed for the power of an angel, the most powerful, heavenly, beautiful creature known. He laid it on his desk and opened it. The inside of the box was gently covered with red matted fur. And in it, laid a delicately carved wand. The print on it was a masterfully cut angel wing, signalling a lot of power. Much more than mine.

"Cast the hovering spell on that box," Harkinsailo said, gesturing to an empty cardboard box resting in a corner. "It will help see if this wand is right." He finished. I wondered if she knew what the spell was. But it was too late to tell her, because she was pointing the wand at the box. Her eyes focused but she said nothing. Didn't say Ellictus. Remained silent. I heard a whoosh and her eyes brightened. I looked at Harkinsailo. His jaw fell open. I knew why as I looked at the box.

It was floating in mid air. That doesn't happen unless you say something. But she was silent. Wherever her wand pointed, the box hovered there. She lowered her wand, lowering the box as well, until it touched the ground, and she stopped the spell.

"So…. er… I got my wand now. Uh… I guess… I'll be leaving now?" She said uncertainly, turning to the door, gripping her new wand tightly. I followed her. Normally, I would have stopped her, but I wanted to get out as fast as I can. But Harkinsailo stopped me instead.

"Nadia! I mean.. girl! You forgot your…?" He started mumbling to himself, trying to remember what she forgot. His memory was working very poorly nowadays.

"your… er… oh yes. Your wand case," he remembered. He tried to throw the case to Skylar, but his arm was also working very poorly. He was throwing it to right in front of his desk. Skylar flew, forgetting to use her "wings" again, diving to catch it before the delicate wood would smash to the ground. Plonk! She caught it just in time.

She shut her eyes and blinked. Again. And once more. For another time. I am guessing that is what miroanalis do when they are surprised. Or shocked. Don't they squeal and dance and smile and laugh when they are surprised? Or was that when they are sad? Whatever. I am not an MS (miroanalis specialist) and I don't understand them, and that's how I want to live my life after this war. I don't need to know about stuff that is not relevant to me or family or fairy friends.

She got up and dusted her dress, clutching the case and the wand in one hand. She adjusted her hair.

"Well… um… Nadia… I um… am leaving now, again and uh… I'll wait outside," She said, eyes wide.

"I'm coming," I replied quickly.

"Nadia, I must speak with you," Harkinsailo said just as I was about to exit. I looked at Skylar.

"I will stay here with your unicorn. You go and do what you want," she said, beckoning for me to turn around. So I did.

"Er… Harkinsailo, is anything wrong?" I asked quickly, hoping that this would be over and I could just leave, knowing there was more important things to be done.

"No, no Nadia. I was just wondering about why your little sister hadn't come earlier to get the… my old memory, covered with cobwebs," he muttered. "Yes… er…. the wand and why of such high power?" His pale blue eyes looked straight into mine. I bit my lip and turned my head to the window. Skylar did look a lot like

Elliah. Long locks of wavy golden hair, pale white skin, blush, small pink lips…

But she wasn't my little sister. She would be the same age but hey! How did he know! He has never met her! I hate assumptions. But I could not tell who she actually was, and Skylar looks nothing like Elliah without the makeup.

Being an Aeroanalis is the reason for the wand, but I just couldn't say, whether I wanted to or not. I looked back to Harkinsailo's white wings with a gray swirl design, and then back to his face. He cocked his head to his side.

"Well?" He questioned me.

"She is not my little sister," I said, after another long silence.

"Who is she?" He snapped back. I suddenly realized how Skylar must have felt during the interview. Confused, scared, uneasy, anxious. Because that is how I had felt then.

"She is my friend visiting from Solaria." I stammered. I needed to tell him that she was not an Aeroanalis.

"Hmm. And the power?" He asked, an eyebrow raised. I looked around desperately. I needed a new excuse.

"She has been studying with Galandor since she was three. She was voted the Expertise in Solaria. She is the fate's daughter of uh… Silicolia," I said quickly. Silicolia is where the angels live and reign. "She is on her study vacation." I added.

"Oh! She… That is why! But if she was-"

"In case you were wondering, she was born and lives in Silicolia, went to Solaria for a study year and became a fate's daughter in Solaria, and spends her study vacations here with Galandor and I," I gasped. I had said that all in one breath.

"Oh… that explains it all. Since the angels tend to her, she needed this wand. But why didn't she have one already?" He inquired.

"She had one, but it malfunctioned in trying a very complicated spell that was cast by an Aeroanalis- I mean, someone like an Aeroanalis, therefore needing a new wand with the power of an Aeroanalis," I said briefly, and I ran out the door before he could ask anymore.

I can lie, I just detest it. I cannot stand it. But lying was the only way to get out.

"Hi Nadia. Um… I kind of practiced that spell I did inside, and uh, it worked. So… uh… where are we going now?"

"We are going to the modern library, not the one we were at before. That was the Library, or to be more specific, the Ancient Library. The Library is full of ancient books of legends and previous delicate and valuable scrolls and treasures, and is the home of Galandor, the keeper, whilst the modern library has books about history, herbs, spell books, realisty, studies, you name it. We are going there to get you a spell book." I said.

"Oh and, um, what is realisty?" She asked, confused. How could she not know what realisty is? Oh, now I remember. They have fantasy.

"To you, fairies and mermaids and angels and wizards are all fantasy, right? But as you can see, they exist. So we have realisty, or Realisticalization, about real life and tales of real people and the miracles made by them although to you they may appear fictional. I believe that below, you call it fairytales, no? Now let's leave." I said, not leaving her any time to answer the question. I flew on to Crystal and Skylar, finally remembering she had wings, tried to use them to fly. But it didn't turn out so well. Her wings flopped and blew her in the wrong direction. "GENTLY FLAP THEM CAREFULLY! DO NOT USE MAXIMUM POWER!" I yelled as loud as I could hoping she could hear. But that didn't turn out so well either. In an attempt to return to me and Crystal, she forcefully pushed her wings, this time blowing her past me and straight into Madame Lesilia's shop, next to Harkinsailo's. They sell beauty products there. Skylar walked out, covered in blush and perfumes and other beauty products. Madame Lesilia wasn't going to be happy with me (was she ever really happy? She seemed so sullen all the time), but she can't get mad at me now. I'm much too busy.

"Um… we can, I mean, can we leave now?" She asked. Then she sneezed.

"Er… I mean, we can go if you…um… are ok?" I said, trying not to laugh. Her face was all pink and she had eyeshadow on her chin and nose. She was hilarious.

"I'm ready when you are," she coughed, flying (without using her wings) onto Crystal. Thank goodness.

Crystal automatically started to gallop, not even knowing where to go.

The modern library, Crystal.

Oh.

She was galloping in the wrong direction. She abruptly stopped and turned herself around. And then she resumed. She galloped past the market place, past the square, but turned around and headed back to the square. I looked directly at Skylar, wondering about what she was doing.

"Nadia?" She asked.

"Mhhm,"

"Uh… when will the war end? I mean, when will it start?" She asked.

"I do not have the slightest idea. Maybe… when you return to the ROC next."

"What should I do with this book?"

"Hmm… I will send you back below, to your home. I would advise you to study and practice performing a few spells, for it will help you in the war. Perhaps it will help you."

"Who said I was going to fight in the war?!" She said, alerted. I was quite confused. She seemed, or maybe she even said, that she wanted to fight with us. Because she was the one who had brought this terrible war to us and poured it on our heads. It would just seem unfair if she didn't join. After all, she did bring the war to us, accidental or not. "Either way, I have not even touched a weapon. When was the last time I used an arrow? How about... NEVER!?" She stated. Before I could answer her silly question, we had approached the modern library.

It was just an ordinary building. Ok, I take that last sentence back. It was an ordinary 3 story building made of glass. Filled with books. It looked as normal as ever, fairies, wizards, librarians and...

"*Gasp*" Skylar finished my sentence.

"Shira!!" She looked astonished. "Up here! In the ROC! But how??"

"Uh... she is a sorceress. She has lessons with Galandor ever so often. She is very talented in the arts of magic. That's the reason why. She has Galandor beam her up." I said, very confused she didn't know. We don't really have secrets here (except for the fact we exist. Duh). Isn't it the same below?

"I didn't realize I was thinking aloud," She muttered. "Shall we go inside?" She asked. But I was already walking in. I walked straight up to the desk.

"Do you have any spellbooks you're giving away? With all spells?" I asked quickly.

"But of course, darling. But I must say, why do you need such a book? Surely you have one of your own." She chimed, looking directly into my eyes. I loved the modern library as much as I did the Library, but the librarians really just are annoying to me. I don't really know why.

"I have my own, she needs it," I replied, pointing at Skylar, who was looking at Shira who was reading a book. "Um… could you please point us to it. I looked back at the librarian, who was pointing at the second floor, to the same section Shira was in. Skylar flew straight up to the section. I caught up with her.

"Why don't you go find the perfect book for me? There is something I have to do." She said. Instead of finding the perfect book for her, I followed her with my eyes.

She walked straight to where Shira was sitting.

"Shira! What are-"

"Casey not now- I mean who are you!!" She gasped.

"Is it really that hard! I'm Skylar, at your service in a good disguise."

"What in the world are you doing here!" She exclaimed.

"Well, that's what I wanted to know from you!"

"I'm not going to tell!" they yelled at the same time. Everyone in the library stopped and looked at them. From the looks on their faces, I could tell this probably wasn't the first time that happened to them.

"Whatever. I don't care at all. Enjoy your joyous reading, and bye," Skylar said. She flew at Crystal speed out the door. Everyone else looked baffled. I knew why. You don't normally see fairies flying at unicorn speed out the door. The fastest fairies are much slower than a unicorn. I just followed her, just as I grabbed the book.

"What was all that about?!" I exclaimed when we got outside. The other people inside were still staring at us through the glass.

"She… she… nothing," she sighed, hopping on to Crystal. "Where to next?" She asked, acting as if she had forgotten what had happened just seconds ago. Those fairies were still looking through the window.

"Home." I said. She looked confused. I pulled out my wand. "Ellictus!" And then Skylar's spellbook was floating in midair. Shira dropped her book and looked at us through the glass. The book followed my wand to Skylar. She grabbed it from the air, and the spell stopped. *"Sylvioa!!"* I yelled, pointing my wand at Skylar and the book she was now holding close to her chest. The transporting spell. Soon her image faded into a bright white flash, the color of the magic, and then she vanished.

Logan

11- The War Begins

I opened the front door to my house and sighed. School was so tiring! Especially Miley. Everyone knows she likes me. I don't get why. I'm just a normal basketball player with dirty blond hair, hazel eyes, normal clothes? If there was a girl I am friends with, it's Stella. But only because she is in my basketball team. No other reason.

Anyways, Miley isn't the only reason I hate school. Math is my main reason. I'm so not talented in that, and Ms. Amherst is just so… um… I don't know? She just gives people the chills.

I checked my watch. 4:30. Wasn't it a Tuesday? Ugh. Basketball. For once in my life, I didn't want to go to basketball. I actually wanted to sleep. I generally never want to sleep, I just don't. But I wanted to sleep today.

"Logan!" Mom's voice called from the kitchen.

"Yeah, mom. I know I have basketball today." I replied hoarsely.

"What I meant was, your basketball thing has been canceled."

"It's not a thing it's a lesson, or you can even call it a session."

"Jeez ok! Well have fun studying math! Your reports will be coming in a month. You need to study harder!"

"Ok, ok!" I said before Mom got into another one of her study lectures. My basketball could also get me a good college!

I sighed and looked out the window, hoping to see a beach again. I used to live in LA, just like Shira. In fact, I went to the same school as her, and I also came to New York in 4th grade. But that's why I wanted to see a beach, not endless skyscrapers and buildings. But if I walked to the other side of the house and looked out the window, I would see the coast. It was a nice place to be at summer, not the beginning of winter. But it looked as sunny as summer outside, and it looked so tempting…

"Logan! Before you go to your room and destroy it with mess, take a shower! It smells like monkeys!" She broke the peacefulness of doing absolutely nothing at all. Whatever. I had skipped going to the PE shower room after PE and just walked straight home, which is an exercise in itself. I live in the suburbs of the city, or somewhere in the outskirts, and the school is urban, in Manhattan.

After I came out of the shower, I saw two things lying on my bed. One was a penny, and the other a dime. I found 11 cents on my bed for no reason whatsoever. I shrugged and picked them off my bed and laid them on my desk.

"Mom!"

"Yes, honey?"

Oh gosh. Marley, my 16 year old diva sister, just came back from singing. She's super annoying, and sometimes I wonder; are girls supposed be like that?

"I've decided I'm going to sing for the annual high school talent show!"

"This is wonderful! Do you know what your going to sing for the school talent show?" Asked Mom with a grin so big I would not be able to speak with that on.

Just as she said that, I walked down the stairs.

"Mom, I'm going to skate around. I'll be back by dinner." I suddenly didn't feel the need to sleep, and I wanted adrenaline.

"Ok, that's fine." She said just as I hopped outside with my skateboard. As soon as I came back I jumped back in because it was sunny but cold. So I grabbed my jacket and came back out to skate again.

"She didn't tell me to stay in the neighborhood, so I'm not," I told myself. I skated past the familiar buildings of the subdivision. Past the bank, the Wellstone school, Shira's home? And in the direction of the school. Soon I approached a very tall apartment building and guess who was there, on a skateboard, and walking a huge dog? Skylar. She stopped abruptly as soon as she saw me. So did I.

"Logan!"

"Skylar!" We said at the same time.

"Uh... what are you doing here?" She asked.

"Um.. I'm just riding around. Is this your home?" I asked, gesturing to the large building towering above our heads.

"Yeah." Then there was a long awkward silence.

"Er... I guess I'll see you tomorrow, if you're not sick. And if you're still alive." She said. I laughed.

"Sure."

"Bye."

"See ya," I said. Well that that was awkward. I'm always a disaster when talking to girls.

I headed further away from the building. When I glanced back, Skylar wasn't standing there anymore. She was flying there.

"*GASP*!! Sky-"

Before I could finish my sentence, she zoomed over, making her much taller than me, and more scarier.

"Don't say a word or even think about it!" She hissed. "This never happened," she said, and then zoomed back towards that building she called home. She paused and took a breath. "And if you do, you will regret it!" She announced, on the ground. And then she disappeared through the front door.

Then I went back.

I had never known Skylar well. I had never tried to know her well. She was just some person. I just made a short summary of her when I met her, and it hadn't changed.

My Summary: Long time in New York City. Brown hair. Green eyes. Not concerned about clothes, like Miley. Not a bubble-brain. Focused. Shy. Clarinet player.

My New Summary: Long time in New York City. Brown hair. Green eyes. Not concerned about clothes, like Miley. Not a bubble-brain. Focused. Shy. Clarinet player. Can fly.

What had happened in the hall this morning, that… she wasn't lying. She could fly, unlike all of us. We're just normal people. That live here. Maybe she had… had… gone somewhere in the sky before. I don't know how long she has been able to fly. If she was born with the ability, which she probably has (considering that her flying was perfect), then obviously she has! And- uh oh. I was thinking about it. I remember distinctly what she said.

"Don't say a word or even think about it! And if you do, you will regret it!"

But no-one took her seriously, so it's hard for me to. I mean, what's the worst she can do? It's not like Shira's suddenly gonna be a wizard and Skylar isn't friends with her anymore but Skylar calls her to cast a forgetting spell on me but she refuses and so she gets her own wand and casts the spell on me and turns out to have a wand even more powerful than Shira's and is a more powerful wizard and then I forget everything that happened? I so don't think so.

So I am just gonna relax. Skylar flies! Big news. I don't care. Skylar doesn't matter. No one does. I just gotta get on with life.

Skylar

I ran straight up to my room and grabbed my iPhone 5c. I frantically scrolled through the contact list until I reached "S". How come everyone's name begins with S?! Then I found Shira. I tapped call.

Brrriiing, Brrrriiinnngg! Brrriiinnnggg brrrrrrrrrrrrrrrriiiiiiiiiiiiiiiiinnnnnnnnnnnnnnnngggggggggggggg!!!!!!! It rang, connecting to Shira. She finally picked up the phone.

"Hello?"

"Shira! I need you to cast a spell on Log-" She hung up. I looked at my phone. It read- call ended. Why? UGGHH! That meant I have to cast the spell! I can't get Nadia, she's mad at me about the war. BUT HOW AM I SUPPOSED TO CAST A SPELL!! I flipped through the spell book lying on my desk. It was alphabetically placed! And in that fairy language! I am so bad with dictionaries.

But wait! There was still a solution. In the shop I just thought about lifting the box and I didn't say anything. Could it be the same? I ran back downstairs, wand in my hand. There was Jason and Ryan. Ryan wouldn't really care, but Jason would, since he's the tattletale and the crybaby. Just what I would need.

I grabbed him by the arm and pulled him upstairs.

"Why are you doing this! I want to play cars!" Jason fussed.

"Stop fussing and follow me," I said and glared at him. He became silent. I pulled him into my room and shut the door. I looked at him. "Did you go to the bathroom?" I asked. I don't want any accidents on my bed.

"Ju-just now, Skylar. Why have you brought me up here? I'm going to go play cars," he said and ran towards the door. But I picked him up and dropped him on my bed.

"You're incredibly annoying, do you know that? Acting like Ryan. PUH leeeease!!" I said. All part of the plan. He would cry and tattletale, but I would do the memory spell. That way it's better for the both of us. And it worked like a charm.

Tears flooded his eyes his mouth opened and just as that happened, my arm extended and my wand was pointing straight at his head. He suddenly flinched and backed away from me. I was confused. Why was he doing this? I wasn't gonna harm him!

"I'm too young to *die*!" He squeaked. Whaaah? Oh yeah, Harry Potter. I rolled my eyes. Harry Potter isn't scary! He is awesome! I AM NOT A WITCH! Whatever.

"I'm not going to kill you, so *shush!*" I shouted. His arms were shaking and his lips were trembling as his jaw opened for another: *Mommy!* Skylar said a bad word! I should have predicted that, having lived with him for 7 years. I was simply giving bait for the fish, as Mom says. I think that means in English: Giving him info to tattletale about. Great. Another reason to cast the spell.

I grabbed his shoulder and pulled him down, and covered his mouth with the other hand. Ryan would have licked it, knowing my weakness, but Jason was just desperately trying to scream. I lifted the hand off his shoulder and grabbed for the scotch tape on my desk. *Plonk!* It fell to the ground. My arm had to stretch to reach it. It felt like twister, the game. The arms twisting and on opposite sides, while I was on my knees. I finally gave up, all frustrated and sweaty, and let go. Finally unstretched, I grabbed the tape while Jason made a run for it. I threw the tape on my bed and turned around, on my knees, to find the door swinging open and Jason scampering down the steps. There was no way I could catch up to him before the "bait" slips out of his mouth. By the time I ran to the doorway, he was already at the bottom of the steps.

I pulled my wand out and imagined him flying. But zooming up the stairs and straight back in my room. When I opened my eyes, he was hovering in the air.

"HELP! Let. Go. Of. Me. Now!!" He said, running out of breath. I pulled my wand backwards and he followed it. Wand in one hand and with Jason floating in front of it in my room, I shut the door as well as the spell. He dropped straight on my soft, large bed. He looked astonished. Well duh it's not a fake wand! And he ruined my neatly made bed. Great (again). All that work for nothing. But I guess that was my fault, too.

I ripped a piece of tape off and covered Jason's mouth with it. I pointed my wand at him and realized just then that I didn't know how much of his memory would be erased. Uh oh. Either he would not remember what happened a second ago, or where he was born. What part of his memory would it have erased? But I would have to give a try. I closed my eyes, wand outstretched, and started to mutter.

"Please work, please work, please work…" I said. I replayed everything that happened in my head, up to the part where my eyes were last opened, and I heard a zap. I opened my eyes, and…

"Skylar, why- what gagged me with this tape? Why am I here?" He said. His eyes were wide with a twisted look on his face.

"You mean, you don't remember coming to this room?" I asked, hopeful.

"No! I was playing cars a second ago, and now I'm here. Can I go?" He asked, also hopeful.

"It worked… IT WORKED!" I yelled, jumping up and down, totally ignoring him. He just slipped out the door. Then I looked directly at my wand. "Good Job wand," I said, then chucked it on my bed.

Just then I walked down to check the mail. We normally don't get anything (or at least I don't) but I was feeling lucky. More nervous, actually. There was a fluttery feeling in my stomach. It was speaking gibberish, so I couldn't understand.

"Shut up stomach. It's just the mail," I told my stomach. Then Mom appeared out of no where.

"Who are you talking to?"

"No-one. Just getting the mail."

"Hmmm. Ok," she said slowly, disappearing the same way she came. That was weird. So I just ran down the steps until I reached the bottom. At one point, I tripped on a step near the 5th floor. So I wasn't in a happy mood when I reached the bottom.

"Ughh… stupid stairs. Always getting in my way," I muttered. I looked at the foggy sky. It was sunny, but it became foggy. Had the war started? Is that why?

Just then, a small slip of rolled paper floated out of the sky. It looked like papyrus. It fell just in front of my feet. I bent down to pick it up. This is what it said.

Oh, Skylar.

The world of magic will see you fail. As you have brought the war upon them. Do they deserve it? Perhaps they do… and perhaps you could defeat me. But don't keep your hopes as high as my power and eternal rule. There is no one on your side. Everyone is hiding in their cottages, with fear and anger and evil, for you. Who will help you? Galandor? Most unlikely. Nadia? What could she possibly do to help you? Even if she could, even if she could, she wouldn't. Even if it would benefit her or her

dead parents. Your a pain up her nose, to her. Anyone else? Don't believe those other fairies will come to the rescue, because they won't. They're rubbish that grew wings and became thicker than the dumbest ogre to ever roam the universe. Don't play at my game. I have control over your mind. I can see what you think. And the little "flash forward" you had was only a millionth of a grain of rice of my power. That is what you will be when you are defeated.

I pried the paper from my eyes. Man, this guy speaks a lot! But if I really do fail, all will be lost. I shivered and forced myself to read forward.

Ha ha ha! I am prepared. Or preparing, as one may say. I have army, thirsty for your blood!

Enjoy your defeat and shame,

Fairy King Elf, ruler of the Skies

I looked directly at the sky, frightened. The sky was no longer pale gray, it was a swirl of dark blue and purple and black. In the middle of the swirl was a dark gray large puff of cloud with red bolts of lightning shooting out. Long bolts of lightning. I ran for my life. I didn't know what poisoned lightning would do to you, but it probably wasn't good. I was sprinting yet it seemed the building was so far away. The note I was clutching started to become heavy and it floated away from my hands. I didn't care. I just wanted to get inside.

Finally I reached the front door. My hand quickly lifted and reached for the door handle, and then ZAP! I felt a burning sensation in my back. And then I fell to the ground in pain. I can't really remember all of what happened next, but I will try to tell what I do.

I could feel my heart stressing to beat. My mind was as blank as ever. All I could see was a land of white. Nothing there. Nothing floating around. No King Elf. Just an endless emptiness.

But then a pair of pointed midnight blue shoes with glowing white stars stepped in. Along with a pair of swirly ribbon ballet shoes. And I suddenly found the energy to look up.

There were two figures standing there. Both taller than me. Their faces were hazy and I was dizzy so I was not able to identify them.

"*Is she alright?*" A voice chimed.

"*No need to worry, Nadia. She is fine,*" an elderly voice replied. I shut my eyes for a few seconds and flopped on my back. I am surprised there was even a floor. I opened my eyes again and blinked two times then everything became clear, but I did not have any strength left. They must have noticed, and they walked towards me so I could see them.

"*Hello!*" The first voice called. I was unresponsive.

"*Resilo! Allisilio ofa heries memorilia ofa thel realm of clouds hasilis beenilia talsiken awailis, alsong witheis heries strenghisilia!*" The second voice said.

"*Oh. I'm Nadia, in case you were wondering,*" she said. Then she realized I still couldn't see and moved right above me. Or flew, to be precise. Then an old man walked around me. He pointed his finger and I automatically stretched into a stiff upright position and I remained like that, but floating an inch above the ground. Since they were both taller than me, they stayed how they were. Then the old man spoke up.

"*I am sorry for not introducing ourselves. This is Nadia, and I am Galandor. We are people that you met earlier in a place called the Realm Of Clouds. But now you have no memory of that place due to the heavy magic force that struck you. So let me start again. You are a human that has the rare ability to fly. In the skies, you are known as an Aeroanalis. You are related to our most beloved king Arraculis who was the most powerful king we ever had and who left the skies to marry a woman of Earth. You are his heir but the only one with the ability to fly in this generation. You had discovered the Realm once, and there you met Nadia. Or, actually, she met you. She brought you to me for help. We soon found out you were an Aeroanalis and let you go back to your home before king Elf could realize your presence in the city. You had returned once more in seek of Nadia's help, but I do not know most of the details from that experience since I was not there. But after you had left the first time, he realized you were once there, and he got prepared to kill. It's because you have the same royal fairy blood in you from Arraculis mixed in your human blood. Your royal connection makes you even more powerful than him and makes king Elf intimidated and he cannot stand this. He also anyways hates humans and loves to see everyone in pain, and he would relish winning over you.*

In all, he is evil, but King by his blood." While Galandor spoke about king Elf, I noticed Nadia looked uncomfortable and was fiddling with her fingers. But then again, who would feel comfortable when he is mentioned. *"So this king has raged a war... to find and erase you. He would kill to keep the secret that you are more powerful and rare and miraculous than he is, for he wants all to believe he is the one."* He said. Then there was a long silence. *"All that live under his reign see you as someone who could create an amazing thing, or create chaos. But not all have the courage to fight against him. So Nadia and I will help, because we see in you a chance of freedom, and not see you as a cause of death.*

I'll give you back your memory, but your strength will be hard to grant, since King Elf's cruel magic is almost more powerful than mine. So in return, I will take grant you with a mild sickness. I'm sorry, but would you rather flop around or fly?" He asked me.

"Fly," I managed to croak with great effort.

"Then I must," he said. He raised his staff at me, and then I don't know what happened, but I found myself lying in my bed. And Ryan sitting on it.

"Mom! Skylar's awake!" He yelled. Then mom rushed up the stairs. And I soon realized why.

"Hey sweetheart, are you okay? Mrs. Taylor noticed you lying on the steps when she was giving her dog a walk ! She called us and we brought you back up here. And oh my, now you have a high fever. But so fast - how? I don't understand... Looks like you need a bit of rest. Lets keep you home rest of the week," Mom said worriedly. YES!! That gave me enough time to finish the war and win it!! But their was one con…

"Skylar, have you drifted off in thoughts somewhere? In case you are getting any ideas, you're most likely going to be in this bed and rest until you recover."

Just then Dad returned from San Diego. Dad had gone on one of his one month business trip, and then it got extended by two weeks. So we missed him so much! And then he came back, it felt like a relief.

"DAD!" Ryan and Jason tackled each other down the stairs in an attempt to meet Dad. When they reached the bottom, Ryan pushed him on the ground and he landed on his face. Then he trampled all over Jason, and got up and tackled Dad. Then I got up and ran all the way down despite my fever.

I ran over to hug dad. It just felt like years and years of not seeing him, rather than a month and a half.

"Skylar, I missed you," he said softly.

"So did I." I replied. Then Mom came down.

"Skylar, you're unwell. Don't worry, you'll get to see Dad. But you have to go to bed," she said. I started to crawl up the stairs. I got under the covers and slept, not even caring it was six 'o'clock and I hadn't had dinner.

****

The next morning, I woke up at 7:30. I guess I was just catching up on my sleep. So I got up, went downstairs, and made my breakfast; plain old everyday cereal. But I couldn't eat it. Something in my head pulled me out of the present and dragged me to the Realm Of Clouds. The pulling thing threw me into the future of the Realm, and then snapped. I saw myself looking at the war birds-eye view. It was like the fairies and wingless fairies, elves, I presume, against trolls. An army of trolls and black dressed elves, short ones, with fangs. The two armies clash together, stabbing and shooting and fighting. I had never seen a war in the flesh, but then again, this wasn't real.

In the center of the war stood Galandor, staff to staff with King Elf. They were shooting spells at each other. And on the side, Nadia had a bow and arrow and was shooting at an elf. Then I swooped down, grabbed Nadia's arrow, and then…

WHOOSSSHH! I opened my eyes and to my surprise saw not a war but an unfinished bowl of cereal. And me in my pjs and not whatever I was wearing at the war. I glimpsed out of the window. It was still dark. It was bright and vivid when I saw the war. I jumped off my chair and walked to the balcony.

A streak of pink lighted the sky. The parts beside the pink was different shades of dark blue. I looked to the east. The top of the sun was about to appear over the lake's surface. I looked closely. The pink was becoming a deep purple, and then BAM! It disappeared! It set! At 7:30 in the morning! So the whole November 1st was 2 minutes! But no… the sun began to creep over the lake once more, and the new streak of pink turned to the orangish glow of the sun, and the sky turned bright blue and the sun was too bright to look at.

I walked back indoors and looked at the computer date. Still November 1st. Oh well. I had fun going out, at least I had felt less feverish, but this was no matter to smile about. Fighting in a war was not a joke. And that was exactly what I did that day.

I ran (even though there was no need to run) upstairs. I grabbed the spellbook and sat down to read it. If I could understand the Fariolas blah language spoken, surely I can read it. I opened the first page.

The print was so… weird. It looked like scribbles. But like magic (which DOES exist) the words slowly fell into place, and after like, 5 minutes, I was leafing through the pages as if it were an ordinary english easy reader book. I was looking for a teleportation spell at first but I realized soon, I don't need that! I can fly! What was I looking for. And I knew that I would need a summoning spell. I was at the "s" section at the moment. I began to scan the pages.

Staring Spell- to stop starers

(Eskilikoso)

Street Stalkers- to drive away stalkers and to clear the streets of stalkers

(Arriliosas)

Success spell- the spell to be successful in small things; cooking food, races, etc.

(Succerisicolia)

Summon Spell- to summon an object (living or not)

(Ellectravincalia)

I circled that and tried to memorise it. All those spells, how could someone possibly memorize all of those spells! They were so complicated! Not to mention the book was at least 8 inches thick, and maybe 4 pounds heavy, but there was 8,000 spells minimum in that book. It was extraordinary, how someone could learn them all. And yet I wasn't able to memorise one.

I was spells muttering to myself when the door creaked open. Mom was standing in the doorway.

"Skylar, are you talking to yourself? Whatever, I just came in here to tell you that the twins (Ryan and Jason) have gone to school, Dad went to office and I'm supposed to go downtown for about 4-5 ish hours for business purposes and erm… you're gonna be home alone. So I have a few rules: No stepping out, no junk food, no calling anyone, and don't open the door or pick up any phones unless you recognise me or Dad, ok? Bye honey!" She said, and then left. She probably didn't want me to reply to her "rules". But I will have to break them anyways. How else would I get to the clouds? (Rhetorical question)

I went to the "T" section of the spellbook again and I found time tartar.

Time tartar- for speeding or slowing time.

(Osilis eg. 19 minutes slower than actual time)

I checked my watch and pulled the curtains aside. Mom was pulling the car out of the curb. Perfect. Just a few more minutes and I was off. I pulled a small brown used hiking backpack from under my bed. I had packed it earlier with stuff I would need; the spellbook and wand, my phone (don't know why), etc. I grabbed it, opened the window, and jumped out.

****

I soon reached the hole in the clouds. There was no barrier that day. I flew straight through, confused, and zoomed all the way to the Library. The door flew open when I lifted my arm to use the knocker.

It was just as I remembered it. And in the center of it sat Nadia and Galandor. They looked frightened, and then pulled me in.

"You have been absent much too long. A letter has been send from the Black Palace. Straight from the Ice

Throne room," Nadia said. I shivered when she mentioned ice. Hadn't I been there before?

"Yes, we must tell her. The war begins in an hour… and we don't have an army-"

"Call everyone you can! Tell every realm! Get an army! Find weapons! It's a Do-or-die, people! Literally," I said, interrupting Galandor. Both of them looked shocked."Go! Now!" I said. I couldn't stand looking at them standing there, looking at me dumbfoundedly. I opened my backpack and pulled out my wand. And with magic, I pushed them out the door.

I sat down and pulled the spellbook out. I needed a finding spell. To find what I needed, and fast; an army. Of elves and fairies. I finally found the spell.

I walked outside. Crystal was still there.

"Run, Crystal," was all I could say.

****

There was not much I could say. But now I was standing in front of an Army. But I didn't feel like myself. And I realized why.

"Oh my gosh! I forgot to set the time changer. I ran to the side and cast the spell. "*Osilis... um...forisilios hoularisium solowerisilia intoilias... Earth*," I said. And I gasped. I didn't know I could speak the language! I just said Osilis... um... forty hours slower in earth. But with all my heart I hoped everything would work, not just the spell.

"BOOM! BOOM! BOOM!" The ground shook rhythmically with the booms. It sounded like an army marching. King Elf was arriving. And everyone around me sensed it. Soon they marched into sight. The clouds swirled above our heads. And we realized, we were largely outnumbered.

We had everyone in 15 realms, every fighter and others, to make and army, but Elf had at trolls that made up for the strength of 50 realms. His army was like an ocean, as far as the eye could see. But we had a positive too. We were fighters and they were trolls and monsters and even tiny elves, about the same height as garden gnomes.

"So..." Elf began as they had stopped marching and he was face to face with Galandor, Nadia, and I, along with a very anxious and aghast and pale army which did not seem like an army of fighters but a flock of chickens.

"I see you got my note... and took it very seriously. But as you see and have noticed you are vastly outnumbered..." He pronounced every word as if it was the most delectable sweetest treat of revenge able to be said. I scowled. But I could not do that without a smile. It was hard to take an evil king who is 3 feet tall seriously. Nadia's eyes narrowed at Elf. Then she glared at me.

Suddenly the sky felt chilly and grey, although only a mild breeze was there. I took in a breath of the dusty air on the battlefield..

"How could you possibly think-"

"Are you done already? We can't stand to hear your voice. And plus, we're kind of waiting for a war to start, but I guess I'll just sit back, have a cup of tea and just watch you tell you're speech 'till midnight. Because I am ready when you are, although, at the speed we're going at, I'm not really expecting a war." I interrupted Elf. A buzz of astonished gasps and mutters and whispers hovered above both armies. I didn't even look at Nadia or Galandor. It was once where I could say something rude or mildly offensive without Mom knowing. But the most funniest part was Elf. He was just standing there, looking like a toddler whose candy had been stolen by some teenagers (me, in this case) and been devoured right in front of him. Except for crying he was standing there, fists clenched, jaw hanging in the balance, eyes in a scowl. Say goodbye to those sweet treats of revenge, and have a taste of your own game!

I couldn't help laughing. Actually it was more like cackling. And I cackled so hard I started having tears. Then I walked up to Elf, who was still in statue mode, and started patting him on the head. "Aaawww, it's ok. You don't have to be scared that I'm going to win the war and your not!" I laughed. The army behind me gasped.

"There's a limit to absurd-ness, especially at a war," one person said.

"King Elf isn't nearly as stupid as this stranger who asked us to fight in a war. And could you believe it's a human!" Another stated. Just then I realized that I have to put the disguise on. I had forgotten that it doesn't automatically come back when I come like the way it dissapears when I leave. I grabbed up a few strands of my hair. Shaggy brown hair, with split ends was all I saw. Actually I don't know what split ends are, but that doesn't matter.

Just then, Nadia grabbed my by the shoulder. I flew up in an attempt to let go, but she just flew up with me.

"What did you think you were doing down there! Wars are meant to be serious, especially when you're leading it! Both armies are down there, willing to fight, but you are not budging. We just want to get this over with, Sky-" I interrupted Nadia.

"I apologize for the previous experiences and am ready to resume the fighting," I said. Nadia's jaw hung open, though I don't see a need for that. Probably the change of mature-ness. I floated back down, since Nadia's arm had fell to her side and she was no longer clutching my shoulder. I turned around.

"Listen, I am sorry about what happened earlier," I said to my army. Then I turned around to face King Elf.

Selina

"Selina! Dinner's ready!" Mom called. I tugged at my earphones and paused the music playing on my iPod. But I put the iPod in my pocket and put the earphones back on and the music began blaring in my ears again. I didn't need to stop listening for dinner.

I trudged down the carpeted steps onto the wooden floor. There was a familiar sight. My mom was standing in the kitchen, doing whatever you do in a kitchen, Dad was watching a Sherlock Holmes thingy mabober, and Jack, my 17 year old brother was slumped on the couch, staring blankly at the TV screen. An occasional yawn would slip out of his mouth. His eyes were half open half shut, and every once in a while he would fall asleep but quickly pull himself back to his usual mode- tired.

My eyes switched to a 2 and a ½ year old Brooklyn, nicknamed Brooke, who was sitting on 2 cushions piled on a seat so she would actually be able to see above the table. As usual, she was just whining and crying and fussing and you-name-it and yelling random things in gibberish. But everyone ignored that.

Soon we were sitting in front of plates of food, and Brooke had her mouth shut. But I couldn't eat. I was just breaking my food into tiny little bits, and breaking those tiny bits in halves. I couldn't stop thinking about Skylar. It seemed like school was the sun, NYC was the solar system, and we were the rocky planets: Shira/ Venus, Faith/ Earth, and me/ Mars. But it felt like Skylar was the last planet in the solar system: Neptune. She seemed so distant, so secret, so cold. Like her heart was frozen and blocking us out.

I wondered what secret stuff she was up to. Sitting down. Talking. Sleeping. Walking. Then again, those aren't very secret things. But she still seemed so secretive.

I still don't know what made me walk away. It seemed like she was pushing us away. I am normally that weird immature person at school. But it's still hard to believe about fairies and wizards that live on a giant cloud. Soon she'll be talking about unicorns that dance on rainbows!

I would have taken it pretty seriously if I was still 6 or something. Fairies are just outrageous for an eighth grader to think about. Just crazy. Boys are even less crazier, which is actually saying something.

"Eat your food quickly Selina, I still want you to have time to work on your NaNoWriMo book. You haven't even started!" She said.

"It's only the first day, and Skylar and Faith and Shira haven't started yet either," I muttered under my breath and took a bite. Skylar just seemed to be coming into everything, including my schoolwork. I got an F in math since Skylar wasn't there, which made me unfocused. I hate being the only one doing things, and it's just Skylar and I there.

"And normal authors write at least 20 pages a day, and we don't have time for that. It seems as if-"

"Nom nom nom!" I tried to make it sound like chewing with my mouth open. "Really good food Mom! NOM NOM NOM NOM NOM NOM NOOOOOOM! Oh wow! I'm finished! Gotta go!" I got up with my plate and dumped it in the sink. Jack looked disgustedly at me. Mom and Dad looked very confused. Brooke was sitting there and enjoying her food. And I took off to my room.

I cannonballed into my bed and pulled out my iPod. I hadn't realized I left my earphones downstairs and the music had paused. I pressed the home button and scrolled through all my apps and hit iMessages. Immediately a text box opened.

Hi Faith. I typed.

Hey Seina. She replied almost immediately.

What's up? She asked.

I dunno. I typed

:(__. Faith sent. That's her thinking sign.

Thinkin about Skylar? I clicked enter. I miss her.

Same here. Faith replied. Shira's becoming friends with Miley.

I know. Skylar used to say she's even less smart than her bubble brain cronies. I said.

Hmmm… Replied Faith Um… I have to do something… TTYL. She said. Then this happened-

Hippie dude left conversation.

I sighed. Faith always has something to do. So I spend my time doing 3 hours homework, 30 minutes eating and another 30 minutes checking texts and emails. And on weekends I do nothing. Or on weekends I go shopping with Shira, play violin, post on my blog…

While Faith goes skiing, traveling, nature clubs, surfing, other clubs like sports club, tutoring clubs, you name it. She's even able to turn in her homework on time.

I wondered what Skylar did at home. She had the same study schedule as me, uses 30 min. to check emails, what else? When I used to go to her house in pre-k, she used to play superheroes. I'd be the one who could breath underwater, and she was the one who could fly. She wanted to play active stuff, like jump around, or run outside, and spray each other with hoses. She'd also want to paint. Not once did she like my suggestion of pretending we were fairies or princesses or rich ladies with painted nails and giant hats and poodles and liked to lounge by pools and sip their pina coladas through straws.

If she could fly, I wondered how long she had known that. Then I would see that she wasn't as bored as I was. I mean, if she could really fly. I mean, I'm using an 'if' because she seemed serious when she said it. She doesn't joke around nearly as much as I do. But if she could really fly, then she was a lucky duck. Imagine soaring through the skies, being able to choose where you want to go, and meeting real fairies! What a dream come true!

Just then, some white magic floated out of the ground, like cloud, and soon it covered me like a duvet. My whole body was immersed in a cloud of sparkly white magic, and then it pulled me out the window...

Skylar

The king was speechless. So I turned back to my army to find Shira, Selina and Faith standing there.

"*Gasp*!" I gasped. They all gasped too, like they didn't mean to be there.

"The ROC... Skylar..." Shira looked directly into my eyes. "Are these armies here? Is this a war?"

"What is going on in here!" Faith and Selina said. Just then Galandor walked behind them. The army behind all of them were choosing weapons. Galandor laid a hand on Shira's shoulder. She turned around, and then looked at me, then back at him.

"Yes, Shira, there's a war. Did you bring your wand?" Galandor asked, completely cool and collected.

"Uh... yes?" She seemed hazed, glancing at her ugg boot. "Skylar, you know him?"

"Mhhhmm," was all I could say.

"Uh... I'll take that as a yes. Both of you have actually been here before?" Faith asked in disbelief.

"Mhhhmm." I repeated.

"Ok, great! But why am I here?" Faith asked.

"I brought you all here because I believed Skylar could use some support from her friends, as all would," Galandor said.

"Now what do I keep missing out on?" Selina joked after a while just as everyone was quiet. "Wings, an ugly looking castle and an ugly looking man to match," she said, gesturing to Elf. None of us laughed at that. "And *is that a rainbow waterfall?*" Selina's eyes twinkled. Same reaction each time.

"Mhhhmm," I said. Shira giggled. Faith didn't.

"All of you who has no idea why you're here," Galandor began. The armies immediately looked here. It was true we didn't tell them why. "Including the army, it is because there is war. Caused by the leader of our group, an Aeroanalis, an offspring of King Arraculis, who has the ability to fly without wings or any extra magic. Now," He softened his voice. "The king believes to rule every independent land, acclaimed or not, in eternal evil, but the earth is full of non believers. Snobbish independent people who roam and cover the planet. So many of them it would be practically impossible to have a reign on even one. So he throws hate at every one of them. But not just earthlings, also any sort of creature with more power than he does, for example, a miracle creature. The Aeroanalis with us here is a miracle child. She has more power in her pinkie finger than everyone Elf could brainwash. Both of these are in Elf's most powerful weaknesses and is more than enough to anger Elf. For this matter he wants to kill her, but all of us as well. " He said.

"Erm... Galandor," Shira began, but Galandor was not finished yet.

"But we know that you could help. I know that all of you brave, heroic fighters have that knot of fear and question and will lodged in you, but for Arraculis, would you have gulped it down? The miracle child standing in front of you does not differ to Arraculis himself in front of you, guiding you through the war as a mighty leader. She is no less. So trust her as if she was him. She is royal. The war is about to start. And you're an army. So you fight. But do you want to fight?" Galandor asked.

The fighters just listened.

"King Elf has tortured, banished, and killed us for nothing. This would continue if we don't win this. We all have a dream- a dream to be free. A feeling to fly free, to be able to soar once more, a longing to smile and feel the joys of life. But what is a dream that will never come true? It's a memory. A memory of something that never happened. If we lose, our future would be the opposite as to if we win the war. But there are prices to winning the war. All the same, would you rather be in debt and pay and suffer your ever so short life, or maybe pay your lives for freedom for your souls to thrive in? And if you are willing enough to sacrifice for others we can win! We will win! The littlest of a person can change the fates of many. Keep everything dearest to you- along with all of your dreams and fight! Fight if you want to see the sun again! Fight if you love your family! It's die in loyalty to Arraculis and for everything you see... or be killed by every form of everything you hate. If we win, imagine it. You will be successful. Victorious. Everything that Elf isn't. You would make Arraculis proud." He said, almost like he would fight for them. Their expressions had changed. Into deciding, I'm- gonna- change- the- world faces, and I finally felt like I had courage inside me too. I felt important and strong, and that everything was gonna be okay. But of course, my friends didn't.

"Skylar, why are we all here? We aren't soldiers!" Faith turned white. "This sounds funny, but I don't have any faith in myself!" She exclaimed. But it was the beginning of a war, so none of us had the heart to laugh. Shira then came back to our group.

"Elf hasn't noticed we're here, you know, three extra humans, so it seems useful to disguise, before he kills us." Shira said.

"No way! We don't have any time to do that! I've done it before, trust me, I fell asleep during it!" I exclaimed. I did fall asleep during the blindfold part.

"Of course we don't have time to do the full blown makeover!" Shira said. "I had nothing to read so I read the spellbook..." I looked at Faith and Selina. Their expressions didn't change when she said spellbook. She must have told them.
"So I read the spell book and I went to an advanced spell called the *desceguidia* spell, or in English, the disguise spell. It's a 2 second spell, but for a very advanced magical being." She said, looking at me.
"Would you do the honors?" She asked me.

"Fine." Was all I said. I pulled the wand case out of my bag then got the wand out of the case.

"Don't you need to know what to say?" Shira asked.

"Nope," I said, and pointed the wand at Shira. I imagined her with... " What do you want to be disguised as?" I asked Shira.

"Uh… a fairy, dressed in faded brown clothes, with a black jacket, boots, preferably laced and pants, with a shield and sword and wand in pocket." She said.

… with the brown shirt and black jacket and laced boots and full length pants and a shield and a sword and a wand in pocket. Soon Shira was wearing all that, with the weapons and purple wings with grey stripes on.

"This is perfect. I just need a ball cap and contact lenses." She said. I then imagined them, and soon a red ball cap fell at my feet, with the contact lenses inside it. While Shira got ready, I turned to Selina.

"So, what do you want?" I asked her.

"Oh, I want…"

After all that disguise stuff, we were standing on the battlefield. And King Elf faced us.

"So… let the war begin, in THREE… TWO… ONE… GO!" Elf yelled.

I suddenly got cold feet and I soared upwards to get away. Shira, Selina and Faith followed. They had already gotten used to their wings.

Together we saw everything - The clash of armies. The endless black army fighting with the white. I wasn't used to such an amazing view of such a scary thing. A war. Every intricate detail was in my sight. The way ten feet trolls lumbered around with axes in hand, chopping everything in view, including the other evil monsters, so I guess they didn't know what side they were on. The way Nadia was able to wipe out a whole row of monsters with one flick of her wand. The way Galandor and Elf were shooting spells at each other. Galandor was about 7 feet tall, and Elf was 3 so it was a funny combination, but the power was even.

I suddenly realized I could do something useful instead of floating uselessly.

"I HAVE AN IDEA!" I yelled over the rambunctious noise of the war. "ARE YOU GUYS GOING TO COME?" They started to come towards me. I pulled my wand out and shot a bolt at at least fifty rows and they all vanished. Shira looked surprised.

"Invisible death," A familiar voice behind us said. "I'm surprised you've learned that spell." All of us turned around to find Nadia there.

"I didn't know it was an actual-" I began. But Nadia wasn't done.

"I followed you here because all suddenly went away and I was worried. But here, let me show you this same spell done this other way - then we must go back," she said.

Then she did the same thing I did, but she selected a huge amount of rows, and POOF! They were all gone. Then Nadia grabbed my arm and flew back. When she let go, I followed after her, along with the others. And when we reached back to our side, we saw something that made my heart skip some beats.

Galandor had his back turned, and Elf was standing behind him, with a sword in hand, and SLICE! Galandor was gone. Dead. Deceased. I didn't think it was true. The armies stopped, and there was utter silence. Nadia was silent, her head buried into her hands. Shira was breathing heavily, as if it ached to breathe. And Faith, Selina, and I just hovered there, eyes wide. That moment is hard to describe. It just felt like… we couldn't breathe. And I don't think anybody did.

Just then, someone from my army sliced through a troll, and the fighting resumed.

12- The Arrow

It seemed so weird when Galandor died… like an aftershock. Nadia flew back down to fight, but I think it was to see Galandor once more. So it was just the four of us in the sky. Shira was still silent, as all of us.

It had been at least a day of fighting, but nobody could tell, because the sky never changed, and all of us were restless.

"If we're gonna help Skylar win this war, we probably have to fight," Shira said. And with that they all zoomed away. Without me. I sighed. It felt like a minute ago, I was at home, doing nothing, not knowing I could fly. And now? I was leading an army to war?

Why was it me. I grabbed a cloud and lay down on it. I felt like I could sleep. But I really could only watch the war. So I relaxed on the little cloud, staring into the even higher gray skies.

"*Skylar! Open your eyes!* " an angelic voice called to me. I opened my eyes and there was an angel. I pushed the cloud away and stood straight.

"Who are you?" I asked, confused.

"The angel of your wand. You have an angel wand, and my angel essence is in your wand. I have come to help you." She said.

"With what?" I asked.

"Killing King Elf, of course. I have sensed for a long time that this war is not going to end. Never at this rate. Look at your friends helplessly yet bravely throw themselves in the war because of you. You started the war, and you must finish it, either by killing Elf or sacrificing your own soul.
I shall bestow upon you a bow and one golden arrow that will not miss it's aim. If you shoot this arrow at King Elf, the whole war will cease. My time is limited, so I must not answer any questions. Here, quickly take this bow and arrow." Her arm outstretched with a bow and an arrow. I quickly snatched them, knowing all will be finished if I don't. And the war was almost done.

I zoomed downwards from the spot I was flying from and almost crashed into Nadia. I pulled her to the side of the war where no-one was fighting, but the she pulled me back up.

"What's going on?" Nadia asked irritably.

"I met an angel and she gave me a bow and a golden arrow but I can't shoot so I was giving it to you so you could do it for me." I said.

"I must not do it. This is something that you, alone, must do." Nadia said. And then she gestured for me to fly away.

My hands were feeling sweaty and slippery when I was carrying the arrow, as if I would drop it and it would break into two. I couldn't focus my eyes on anything, but I forced myself to.
I took a deep breath. This would be it. I would shoot, Elf would die the way evil kings do die, and all would be finished. I was already going to be done. But how could I?
I held the bow out, probably the wrong way, but that would not matter.

I took my aim, and I shot. The arrow pierced the air, and landed in the heart of Elf. The war had stopped once more. But this time it wouldn't start again. Elf was a mound of ash on the ground, which blew away in the wind. And his army had disappeared with him.

Nadia stood on a ledge above the war, where everyone could see her, and she said:

"WE WON THE WAR! Thanks to Skylar, the leader of the war. She didn't want to fight, but she fought anyways, and killed Elf with a Angel Wand. And she won the war for us. Everyone may return to their realms, and spread good news." Nadia finished. All the magical beings fighting in the war went home. Except for the ones that stayed here, and my friends.

Just then, the mayor of the Realm Of Clouds stepped out of nowhere whatsoever.

13- A New Life And Beginnings

"I saw the war. It was so amazing how you defeated Elf. But now, we have no ruler." I couldn't help but not liking him under my breath. All he cares about is a ruler? They could make this realm a free country.

"So we have come to make a decision for a ruler. We have been studying the blood maps, and the Aeroanalis would seem the only reasonable choice." He said.

"Why don't you choose someone whose name you actually know?" I snapped back. "Show me the blood maps." He pulled a folded piece of paper out of his pocket and handed it to me.
I unfolded the actually huge paper. It was basically a royal family tree. I studied it. It didn't have my name anywhere. But it had Nadia's.

"I showed it to Nadia. She didn't believe me.

"What do you mean? That can't be me." She said, but her eyes flooded with tears.

"Look here," I said pointing to her name on the map. "That is you. Those are your parents, your mom's parents, and your grandmother's dad. So your great grandfather. Now, your great grandfather from your mother's side was the brother of King Korniculus, who was ruling at the time. But since there was nothing wrong with the family at the moment, the line continued and your family was pushed aside, But there was some problem that had occurred in the next generation, so Elf's family was taken into notice. But since Elf had no family, yours is the one to rule. And you're the current ruler. See my family, my family is in the ancient royal bloodline. It wouldn't make sense to make a human Queen." I said.

"My parents are dead, with my sister. I never had a brother. So when I get married and have kids... my last name would change unless I marry a royal, of which there are none." Nadia said.

Then the mayor spoke up.

" That's not half true. If a villager marries a female royal, his name automatically changes. Only if necessary, though, by legislation." He said. I looked back at Nadia. She had nothing to fight with.

"Then it is decided. I am queen," She said, after a long silence, practically crying with joy. All the villagers of the Realm of Clouds had come out to hear, and they cheered when they found out. Even Shira did. But Faith and Selina were confused.

"What do we-"

"Before a coronation," she said, and everyone listened since she was queen. "I want to make one request, that a statue of Skylar, the one who won the war for us, be put in the square as a memory to her for saving us, and because she may not return." Astonished gasps rose from the citizens, as well as the mayor. Then I began to talk.

"Coming here frequently and being human would not result well. I have many things to do in the human world and being here at the same time doesn't work. People had already become suspicious, and if I tell, this world would not be secret, as it best is. The people would launch tests and come in Airplanes and capture you for stuff you're better off not knowing about. So staying where I should would be better for both of us. " I said. They seemed like they understood.

"Well, I suppose that means you have to leave now. Do you need any help in going home?" Nadia asked.

"I think we're fine," I said. Selina and Faith looked like I had patted Elf on the head all over again. Shira didn't. She pulled out her wand.

"*Sylvioa!*" She said. And with that she was gone.

My friends looked at me crazily.

"How in the world are we gonna get home?" Faith said. And I replied to that with a question.
"Girls, how would you like to fly home. Good." I said, not even listening to what they had to say. Selina squealed. Faith's eyes were wide. I pulled out my wand, imagined them flying and… when I opened my eyes, we were zooming home together.

****

Time hadn't even changed by one minute since I left, in fact, I found myself looking at my mom pull out of the driveway.

I couldn't stop thinking about how short everything was. And how hard it was to
believe it was all true. Everything happening was like a blur- something whizzing past my face. It was there, then it wasn't, like fireworks. I summarized everything that happens in 2 sentences.

I realize I can fly and my flying powers take me to a magical place in the sky with fairies and wizards and angels and evil kings. I accidently bring a war to that place and I kill a fairy named elf and the war ends and I find out I'm royal and someone who is apparently in a distant relationship of mine becomes queen.

I can't believe the climax of my life was just so… short. Riding a rollercoaster is not even anything compared to that. But I'm also nothing. Nobody knows about this. I'm royal, but not at school. I survived a war, but what about 8th grade? Life will be ordinary again, as ordinary as seeing your own finger.

Before I knew it, I was sitting down on the ground at the library (at school) during study hall with a sketchpad. And I had no idea what to draw. So I began to draw the whole Realm of Clouds as I first saw it. I was sketching everything I saw. Every little detail. The designs on the wings of fairies, the waterfall, even the shops.

A whole crowd gathered around me as I sketched. Shira and Logan came too. And when Shira saw it, she smiled. "Old memories…" She said, and Selina laughed.

The End

This book is exactly 28,057 words long and has 144 pages exact.

ABOUT THE AUTHOR

Avni Madhwesh was born in Kansas, USA and currently lives in Switzerland with her loving parents and her little sister. Her hobbies are writing, reading, drawing, and music. She gets most of her inspiration from dreams and makes books off of them. She has been writing since the age of 5 and this is her first published novel at the age of 11.

30229017589929
F MAD
Madhwesh, Avni A.
Just like wings /

Made in the USA
San Bernardino, CA
05 August 2014